CRYSTAL'S SONG

CRYSTAL'S SONG

MILLIE GRAY

BLACK & WHITE PUBLISHING

First published 2011
by Black & White Publishing Ltd
29 Ocean Drive, Edinburgh EH6 6JL

1 3 5 7 9 10 8 6 4 2   11 12 13 14

ISBN: 978 1 84502 340 9

Typeset by RefineCatch Limited, Bungay, Suffolk
Printed and bound by Cox & Wyman, Reading

Dedicated to Celia Baird

The author's thanks go to:
Gordon Booth for his editing and advice;
Martha Booth for her encouragement and support;
and for sharing their memories of a Leith childhood and a
Leith long gone, my grateful thanks to my sisters Mary
and Margaret and my friend Celia.

PART ONE

1

"You've got lots to do, Senga. You really need to get a move on!" urged Phyllis.

Senga shivered as she began pulling a jumper over the summer dress she was wearing. "I know, but I'm that feart, so I am."

"Feart of going out in the snaw?" replied Phyllis as she tried unsuccessfully to raise herself up.

Wincing, Senga picked up a towel and neatly rolled it up before lifting her paralysed sister's head and gently placing the towel under the pillow.

"That feel any better?" she asked pleadingly. But when Phyllis nodded and smiled, the gesture only served to make Senga feel worse. She'd felt so badly now about having blamed everyone for her having rickets as an infant. These rickets, unfortunately, had resulted in her left leg bending outwards. Bandy-legged they called her now but nevertheless her bandy leg worked. Then beautiful Phyllis had been struck down by polio two years ago. Senga's sense of guilt had deepened even more when Phyllis returned from hospital and it became evident that she would never be able to move freely. She'd never run a message, never skip, nor ever play peevers again. Only nine years old she'd been then – and Senga had heard all those whispers that her elder sister wouldn't . . . But Senga refused to let her mind dwell on these sad predictions – after all, people had once said she herself would never walk, yet now she did.

"Naw, I'm no feart o' the snaw. It's that bloomin'

attendance officer coming here the day that's giein me the heebie-jeebies."

Phyllis chuckled. "Look, Senga, it'll be okay. He'll no expect to see you this week after me telling him you'd been smitten with the bubonic plague."

"If only I had been, life would be a lot easier."

"You think so?"

"Aye, 'cause I'd hae been bricked in where he couldnae get at me and tak me aff tae the bad lassies' school." Senga became wistful. "Wish we were still living across the lobby frae Granny Kelly."

The two sisters fell silent. Both were remembering how it was Phyllis catching polio that had got them out of the slums of West Cromwell Street. Aye, the authorities were adamant that they wouldn't allow Phyllis home from hospital until there was a guarantee of satisfactory sanitary conditions. And in no way did the family's rat-ridden and bug-infested single-end in condemned West Cromwell Street meet the minimum of those standards – especially when it was noted that they only had a cold water tap and access to a communal lavatory which they had to share with forty other people.

Yet, if she was being truthful, Senga would have to admit she did so like staying in Restalrig Circus, where every house had three rooms, a large kitchen and a bathroom. It was a whole world away from West Cromwell Street. Most of all she loved the garden and before her father had been called up, he'd kept it all so nice, planting vegetables, fruit and flowers. But Mum . . . well, Mum was just Mum. Senga grinned, thinking that now the ground was covered by four inches of snow her garden looked so beautiful again and no different from anyone else's!

A loud drumming on the outside door alerted the girls.

"Quick!" whispered Phyllis. "Hide under my bed."

The bed in question was a long, topless, coffin-shaped wooden structure on wheels. The wheels had been fitted to make it easier to move around the house – and even outside into the fresh air – but to be truthful, since Tam their father had left, it was still too cumbersome for slightly built Senga and Johnny, her strapping but gangling ten-year-old brother, to manoeuvre easily.

Senga had just squeezed herself under the bed when the rapping stopped, the door opened, and a voice called out, "It's no the rent man. It's only me."

"Oh, it's just you, is it, Etta?"

"Less o' the *just*," teased Etta, squinting at the bed. "You lost something, Senga?" she went on, as she expertly fished Senga out of her hiding place.

"Naw. I thought you were . . . well, you surely ken I'm on the run."

Etta smiled. This dramatic retort was what she expected from Senga, whom she judged to be the least intelligent of the Glass children and was therefore always being kept off school to help in the house. The excuse offered by Senga's mother, Dinah, was, "Well, don't I have to go out working? Not to mention entertaining the troops?"

Since moving into Restalrig Circus two years ago, the five Glass children and their mother had built up a close friendship with Etta and her husband, who lived just over the road, on the posh side of Learig Close. Etta's husband, Harry, had also been called up and was now based with the RAF at Pitreavie over in Fife, leaving his childless wife to look after his aged father, Jacob. The old man and his wife had adopted Harry as a baby and, after Jacob's wife had

5

died fifteen years back, it had proved quite hard for the widower to cope with the somewhat wayward teenager that his adopted son had become. So Jacob was greatly relieved when, some twelve years ago, Harry had courted and then married Etta, a naïve young country lass. The Glass family now knew Etta to be one of those gentle children of nature who had never a bad word to say about anyone, yet was essentially unable to cope with many of the harsher realities of working-class life. Etta had proved to be a real blessing to the Glass family since she simply assumed it was her duty to come in at all times to look after Phyllis. Not that Etta ever did any *hard* housework – after all, she didn't do it in her own house so why should anyone expect her to do it elsewhere? More importantly, what she did do, most successfully, was keep the children company and tell them innumerable stories while chain-smoking any kind of cigarette she could lay her hands on.

"Now, I've fed Phyllis her porridge, Etta," Senga quickly announced, as she began to pull on a pair of Wellingtons. "And if you could just stay here till I get back – I won't be long."

"You won't?" said Etta, half-regretfully: she didn't care *how* long Senga was going to be.

"Naw. I've just to get our alarm clock out of the pawn . . ."

"Getting something *else* out of the pawn?"

Senga flinched as she went over to the coal scuttle and dragged out a canvas bag which clinked loudly as she swung it up on to the tabletop. "See when I went and got the blankets out last week I didnae half get a right red face when Mr Cohen bawled out that he disnae like getting his money," Senga looked around to make sure she was not being overheard before whispering, "in penny dribs an drabs!"

"Aye," countered Etta, "things haven't half looked up since your Mammy got yon job on the buses."

"That's right. And d'you know this, Etta? When she's no had time to collect aw the folks' fares and gie them their tickets, she just stands at the door and clicks the machine as they get aff the bus while they're dropping the pennies intae her hand," confided Senga. "What else can she do but bring the money hame? She doesnae want to lose her job for no doing it right, does she?" Etta made no comment but lit up a cigarette, so Senga felt she had to justify her mother's actions and hurriedly continued, "Besides, between the bus fares and Daddy never seeming to get laid off work for a day or two now he's in the army – which means we get his full pay every week . . ."

"Senga! It's not pay. It's an army marriage allowance," Phyllis emphasised as she corrected her sister, who she considered was always needing help to get things right. "And do you know," she continued, turning to face Etta, "our Daddy even told them to send on another nine shillings from his allowance to us every week?" Phyllis sighed and wiped a tear from her eye. "And that means he's probably not left himsel' enough to buy a packet of fags."

Etta drew on her cigarette again before looking dis-dainfully at the broken stub. "Well, if he's like me and can only get his hands on these awful Turkish Pasha fags he's better off without them." She now pulled some tobacco from her mouth before flinging the dog-end in the fire.

"Anyway, it doesn't matter if it's called pay or allowance," Senga protested. "Daddy's money comes in every week, so things are getting better."

"And Etta, ken something else? Senga's to get a *whole* half pound of Spam and a big tin of Heinz beans from the store for our tea." Phyllis as usual felt she had to butt in to help Senga, yet couldn't resist licking her lips before adding, "And she's also to get a whole bob's worth of chips from the Chippie to go with them!"

"A *whole* twelve pennyworth?" teased Etta.

Senga nodded. "But forbye the Pawn, the Store an' the Chippie, I've got to go and see Granny Kelly to tell her not to wait for Mammy on Friday night as she'll not be going to chapel."

"No got anything to confess?" asked Etta, who knew that Friday night was Confession Night. Senga's head dipped briefly in agreement. "Right! Off ye go."

Etta then turned towards Phyllis. "And now, ma wee dollie-dumplin', how does a wee bit hot toast smothered in best butter sound to you? And all washed down with some nice sweet tea, of course."

Senga didn't have a pixie hood but she did possess a scarf that Granny Kelly had folded in two and sewn up part-way to look as if she had. Then, bending her covered head into the driving blizzard, she muttered, "Blast this snaw!" as she hirpled her way along Restalrig Circus towards Hooper's Aw-thing Shop – which did literally seem to sell anything and everything. There were even rolls of salt fish inside the lower edges of the window and in summer these always proved a happy hunting-ground for swarms of bluebottles. And as for old Mr Hooper's apron, that was indeed an advert for *Before Persil*. On that account Senga was not allowed to buy from Hooper's very often. Yet Hooper's three grand-daughters (for whom he'd taken responsibility when his distraught daughter arrived home after having been deserted by her ne'er-do-well husband) all attended the Mary Erskine Merchant Company school, where every pupil had to wear uniform – straw hats and gingham dresses in the summer; and, in winter, nap coats and long black stockings, held up by proper suspender belts and not tight, itchy elastic bands.

By now Senga was going past Hooper's and was about to walk down Restalrig Road when she luckily turned the corner just in time to see the small No.13 bus that ran between Ravelston in the west of the city to Bernard Street in Leith. Surely, she thought, with the weather being so bad and her having to keep from getting her bad leg broken, not to mention (the most important issue) being seen by a lurking attendance officer, wasting a penny on a bus journey must surely be permitted!

As she began to hobble quickly towards the bus stop, Senga gestured wildly to the driver, only to discover that it was an old friend, Joe Armstrong, who now had taken both hands off the steering wheel and was gaily waving to Senga. Though the bus seemed totally out of control by this point as it hurtled towards her, Senga knew well that it was only another silly prank on Joe's part, and as the bus shuddered to a halt she simply giggled. It was just like Joe to clown in that fashion. He and Senga's mother had at one time been in service together on a wealthy estate, Joe being chauffeur and Dinah the table maid. The Abbey family for whom they worked had always insisted that Joe pick up Dinah at the railway station in Melrose when she returned from her day off. And so the two became and remained very good friends. Indeed it was widely believed that Joe fancied Dinah – but that was only to be expected, since every man in the neighbourhood was attracted to her. Dinah, however, belonged to a devout Catholic family who had sent the young woman away into service solely to keep her away from Tam Glass, her Protestant boyfriend – all to no avail because, despite the objections from both families, Dinah and Tam married and (in Senga's opinion, together with that of all of her siblings) had lived happily ever after.

Once Senga had scrambled aboard the bus, Joe half-turned in his seat and called to his conductress, "That bairn there is yin o' Dinah Glass's."

"So ah'm supposed tae gie her a free hurl, am I?"

Joe winked and the bus took off down Restalrig Road and then across Leith Links. However, just as they were approaching the Leith police station, Senga got up.

"No going the whole way then?" the conductress asked.

Senga shook her head. It was true she could have gone on to the terminus in Bernard Street but what Joe and the conductress didn't know, and she wasn't going to tell them, was that she had business to do in the pawnshop in the ancient Kirkgate. Oh yes, the skin her Mammy was making off her work on the buses was making life so much easier for the Glass family. Besides, she preferred to walk there and then wander into the Old Tolbooth Wynd because of all the odd characters and raw life there that she felt to be part of her own early childhood. She smiled to herself, remembering the Maltese lady with the monkey on her shoulder, the three-fingered knife grinder and the old sailor who hobbled about on a peg-leg. Never would you see such figures in Bernard Street: that was now for the wealthy shipping agents and bankers – men in smart suits and bowler hats.

It cost Senga only two shillings and tuppence to redeem her clock but paying even that small sum mostly in pennies seemed enough to anger Mr Cohen and he warned Senga not to come back next week and uplift her mother's Jigger coat with anything else but siller! Senga was sorely tempted to retort that she wouldn't be back next week as she and her older sister, Tess, and her brother, Johnny, were all being evacuated – mysteriously being taken off to some faraway place called Lasswade that no one had ever heard of.

Almost before she knew it, Senga had reached West Cromwell Street where families were still huddled together in single-ends or room-and-kitchen houses and had to endure sharing the lavatory with several other families. Literally dozens of folk could be using it – how extremely inconvenient that had been, mused Senga, when you were in a desperate rush, because you always had to ask Granny Kelly for the key. Senga had asked her Granny why they kept it locked and Granny had explained that locking it ensured that only the forty or so people entitled to use the lavatory did so – and that no common Tam, Dick or Harry had access!

West Cromwell Street was set on the corner of Admiralty Street beside an enormous pigs' bin where, ever since the war had started, everybody was required to deposit their vegetable peelings and unwanted food. The local children all loved sitting on top of the bin because it looked straight into a very hot and noisy garage workshop where flames and shooting sparks from the forge offered a constant firework display. The most charismatic of the welders there was a man they all called Fiery because not only did the fiercest flames come from his acetylene torch but his clothes constantly required dousing with water when they, too, caught fire. For Senga, however, the real attraction of Fiery was the way he would come over at his lunch break and sit beside the children on the pigs' bin, entertaining them by playing his melodeon – invariably accompanied by his apprentice on the mouth organ. The music provided by this talented duo would instantly have the children singing and dancing ecstatically. Then all the harsh privations of wartime seemed not to matter in the slightest. Adults too, like Senga's mum, appreciated Fiery just as much and he was such a great musician that every Friday and Saturday night he would be found playing his accordion at the Corner Room dance-hall in North Junction Street. Many sailors went there in the hope of picking up a girl and when the interval arrived several of them would liberally buy pints of beer or nips of whisky for Fiery. By the time the interval was over, quite a few of the sailors would be growing a bit fou and a punch-up was likely to ensue. Then the ever-cautious Fiery would carefully remove his precious glass eye and wrap it in his handkerchief before placing it safely in his pocket.

After being suitably entertained from her vantage point on the corner and thinking that one day she would learn to play the squeeze-box or moothie, since they both looked so easy to play, Senga made her way up to No.6 where her Granny and Granddad Kelly lived.

She was glad it was early afternoon because Granddad, who always bad-mouthed his daughter and was forever declaring that Phyllis having been struck down with polio was a clear sign of God's vengeance on her and Senga's father for having entered into a mixed-faith marriage, would still be working or, more likely, propping up the bar of the Black Swan pub. But Granny Patsy Kelly was just so special – and she always made you feel that you were the most important person in the world to her. Her soft Irish lilt brought a deep sense of peace to Senga even though she knew that Granny Kelly was sorely tried by Dinah, her only child and Senga's mother. It had been a heartache for Patsy that her first four children had died as soon as they were born and so when Dinah came bawling into the world she was absolutely elated. Maybe because of that she'd spoiled her but wasn't that quite understandable? She didn't give her husband, Danny, any slack, however. She might just be pint-sized at five-foot-nothing but she was a true matriarch. Senga had listened so often to the tale about how Danny thought he would do just as his work-mates did – go straight to the pub on pay night and let Patsy wait until he took his feet out of the sawdust. Danny had tried it once and was surprised when his blonde, curvaceous, attractive blue-eyed wife kicked open the pub door, skipped over to him and said, "Right, where's the pay packet?" while she flexed her hand menacingly.

Danny had responded by roughly pushing her hand away. "You'll get what's left when I decide to come – and that's *if* I decide to come hame."

"That right? And you'll get . . ." she responded as she raised her hand to hit him.

"Look, Danny," the barman intervened. "Tak oot your pocket money and fling the rest at her. Ye ken, if ye gie her the bloody nose she's asking for, we'll end up wi' the polis in here."

"Look, sonny boy," Patsy sneered, "if he tries slapping me he'll end up sleeping on a slab while Alex Stoddard shrouds him."

"That right?" cackled the barman, as he enticed all the men in the pub to join him in jeering at Patsy.

Unperturbed, Patsy now individually eyed each of the

men in the bar by turn and her steely stare silenced every one of them. "That's better," she said, flinging back her head when the cat-calling stopped. "And don't any of you forget that I'm the daughter o' the prize fighter, Shaun O'Leary!"

From that day on, Danny Kelly always went home with his weekly pay packet which he handed over to Patsy *unopened*. Once she had opened the packet she gave him his pocket money and then he went off to put his feet in the sawdust. Senga knew that, for all Granny Patsy's waspish tongue and fierce demeanour when dealing with Granddad Danny, she had a soft streak when it came to dealing with her mother Dinah, willingly taking on all her responsibilities. And of course, for her grandchildren she would have readily lain down and died. Oh aye. Wasn't she always saying, "The very reason for living – so my grand-bairns are."

On entering the house, Senga was immediately greeted by a big grin from her Granny who leapt across the floor and grabbed her in a tight embrace. "Gosh! Are you not a treat for sore eyes!" But then she quickly released Senga and asked, "Why are you not at school, my lass?"

"Mammy says it's more important for me to look after Phyllis than trying to keep up with the class. And then there's Elsie to see to when she gets back from nursery."

"Aw, aw, aw, aw," groaned Patsy, shaking her head. "Look here, lassie, you need to get an education. Surely you don't want to be like your Daddy and no be able to read or write?"

Senga just shrugged. She had missed so much schooling by now that there was word of her being put in the duffers' class and she knew that was what would certainly happen – provided she wasn't sent off to the bad girls' school first.

"By the way, I met your Granny Glass in the pork butcher's queue the day and she was asking if there'd been any word yet from your Daddy?"

Senga shook her head. Poor Granny Mary, she thought. Just like Granny Patsy, she was small in stature but she was so thin, careworn and round-shouldered that she always looked ten years older than her years. She was regularly bullied by her husband, Jack Glass, a big strapping scunner of a man. And, to add to her problems, he always stayed so long in the pub on pay night that there was very little of his pay left when he staggered out. The lack of a decent share from Jack's earnings resulted in Granny Mary taking on any jobs she could get. She did anything: scrubbing stairs, washing, ironing and looking after bairns. And as if a bad husband, whose gas she couldn't put in a peep, was not enough for her to be going on with, she also had one son, Billy, who was a jail-bird, and another who wasn't quite the full shilling. And as luck would have it, the one she was so proud of, Senga's dad, Tam, was now missing in France. Senga sighed, thinking how daft it was for Granny Mary to ask if there was any word from her dad, when she well knew he couldn't write. It was only then she remembered that she hadn't told Granny Patsy how the war was catching up with them and, come next Monday morning, she, Tess and Johnny were all to be evacuated.

On hearing this, Patsy nodded thoughtfully. "Not a bad thing. Not a bad thing at all. You three being away means your mother will have to stay in at night – and you'll get some proper schooling in reading and counting."

Senga just nodded before realising it was high time for her to tell Granny that Mammy had nothing to confess this Friday – or (to be truthful) nothing she would really want

Father O'Riley to know about! However, before summoning up all her courage by taking deep breaths, she looked around the room and noticed the brown paper bag on the dresser. "Good," she thought to herself. "Granny Glass has sent us a bag of Crawford's Rich Tea broken biscuits. That'll please Phyllis. She just loves having somebody dunk them in tea for her."

2

Tam Glass, his long thin bones aching in the blazing sun, was finding it hard to resign himself to his fate. Here he was, at the age of thirty-two, seated on the hard paving stones of a French village square and faced with the certainty of captivity. "How long did they say this business would last?" he asked himself. "Last year they told us it would all be over by Christmas." He laughed bitterly. "Aye, that was just what they said in the last war, but Christmas 1914 came and went. It didn't end till November 1918 and there were millions dead or maimed afore they declared a cease-fire!"

"Tam!" The voice of young Eddie broke abruptly into Tam's train of thought. "How d'you think it'll go for us?"

Eddie was a mere stripling of nineteen years, whom Tam had befriended from the very day they'd joined up. So close had they become that Tam now knew a great deal about Eddie, who had grown to have complete trust in the older man. Tam soon learned that the young fellow had been adopted and reared by an elderly couple who felt it was their Christian duty to drum the fear of God into him – but he knew nothing about the lad's birth mother. No doubt Eddie himself was completely in the dark on that subject. All he'd ever said was that he'd been quite lonely before he met up with a lassie called Betty at the Church Youth Group. Now that his adoptive mother was dead, Betty had come to be Eddie's sheet-anchor in life and it was his firm resolve to marry her (if only she would have him) because she was so beautiful and vivacious.

Tam chuckled when he heard that. It was obvious that a handsome young fellow like Eddie was a catch that any sensible girl would jump at – even a much sought-after redhead, as Betty must surely be from Eddie's enthusiastic description. Tam's mind went back to the lad's question about the war and he wondered if he should speak the truth and say that he simply didn't know how they'd be treated as prisoners of war and that he too was every bit as shit-scared as his young pal. But before he could answer, the voice of authority boomed out: "Right now, my lads! Stack all your rifles here by the wall. The last-ditch defence is over for us."

Tam nudged Eddie and they both stood up to obey the order from Sergeant Fred Armstrong, the most senior soldier left with the rearguard.

Andrew Young, who preferred to be known as Andy, stayed firmly seated on the ground and, instead of obeying the order, gallantly squared up to the sergeant. "Are you telling us Royal Scots, who are the First of Foot – Right of the Line –"

"– and the pride of the British army no less," butted in Charlie Tracey, who in turn was interrupted.

This time the continuity was broken by George McIntyre who added zealously, "And with us being the oldest regiment in the British army, and well-known to have been Pontius Pilate's own bodyguard to boot, you're wanting us to surrender like a bunch o' yellow-livered cowards, are ye?" George then looked contemptuously towards the English squad.

Fred shook his head wearily. "Look here, lads. It's no about being seen as cowards – it's all about survival! About living to fight another day – when we will win!"

"But we could make a stand right here," protested George.

"Now, let's just get this straight. There are seventy-five of us men here, and that's counting the twenty-four English and Welsh lads. Most of you are raw recruits and we've only got some pesky rifles whose ammunition is running out. So d'you really think we could take on three crack infantry divisions who'll be backed up by at *least* a hundred German tanks manned by battle-hardened experts?"

The men all looked from one to the other. Some had felt quite proud to be the expendable flank that would take on and delay the enemy so that the greater part of the British Expeditionary Force could retreat to Dunkirk and await rescue there. Others were seething, feeling they'd been sacrificed and abandoned by all their officers without a backward glance; and, as Charlie had remarked: "Look, if a hundred thousand gutless French, who're waitin' at Dunkirk to do a bunk, dinnae think their country's worth fighting for – then why the hell are *we* still here?" Every man there nodded his head and voiced agreement.

Most of the men, like Tam Glass and young Eddie Gibson, had been called up in December 1939, and had been given the very minimum of basic training before being shipped off to France on 19 April 1940. What was so galling was that word had spread through the ranks that the British High Command already knew the defence of France was a lost cause! And now here they were, being ordered to capitulate and submit to the glorious but merciless Third Reich, just as the French had done!

Fred was running a quick eye over his men when he discovered young Billy Morrison was missing. "Where in the name of heaven is Private Morrison?" he bellowed.

"Fraternising with some French chick, for sure," suggested Tam with a chuckle.

"The one in Rouen?"

"Aye, Sarge. And she'll be his *ruin* afore lang, nae doot," quipped Tam, who was still highly amused.

"But how on earth did he get there?"

"Billy came across an auld motorbike – and bein' such a handy wee bloke got it goin' again in nae time – an' the last we saw was him riding off some wye yonder," chipped in George, pointing vaguely westwards.

The sudden rumble of approaching tanks silenced everyone. Men prayed silently; some crossed themselves; all stood up straight as the usual German calling-card of gunfire heralded the enemy's arrival. Unnerved by the barrage, eight of the English lads grabbed their rifles and decided to make a dash for it into the cornfield that bordered the village. "Dinnae dae that!" Fred shouted as loud as he could. "If you're caught with guns at the ready they'll mow you down. Come back here! It's useless to make a stand. Believe me, I would take them on if I thought we could win – but I ken it's useless!"

The men ignored Fred's plea and disappeared into the field just as the first tank loomed into view, flanked by a platoon of infantrymen. "Raise your hands, boys," ordered Fred.

"Might as well," conceded Tam. "'Cause let's face it, lads. We've been shafted an' the bloomin' war's over for us."

Eddie nodded. "See, if anyone had telt me when we were called up that six months later we'd be throwing in the towel somewhere in the middle of France – what's the name of this blinking wee place, onyway?"

"Mauquenchy. Just outside Rouen," said Fred knowledgeably.

Once the foremost tanks had taken up position on either side of the square and the German infantrymen were grouped around them with their rifles at the ready, Tam noted that they had left a straight open corridor. He was just about to remark on this to Fred when a jeep-type vehicle driven at speed appeared on the horizon and eventually halted abruptly a few feet from the capitulating British. The driver, whom Tam judged to be a batman, jumped from the vehicle and ran to open the door for the German Oberleutnant, Gunther Wengler. Tam could do no less than admire the man. He was, without a doubt, what the Führer wanted the world to acknowledge: that German officers were all fair, pure-bred Aryans, who wore the Third Reich uniform with panache. In Gunther's case it was more than mere swagger, for he strode with an air of military resplendence, yet always seemed both cool and debonair. The desired effect was heightened as he rhythmically whipped his cane upon his highly polished boots.

Gazing at the immaculate officer, Tam thought, "Aye, son, you may have a batman to press your uniform, spit and polish your boots and run your bath, but are you as lucky as me with a lovely Dinah at home?" Instinctively, Tam felt under his armpits where sweat from a long overdue wash mingled with the exudation of the panic he was trying to keep in check. To keep himself under control, he let his mind escape into a dream-world where his thoughts were back home with his beloved Dinah. A sly smile came to his face when he remembered how every Saturday night she would get into the bath beside him and wash the weariness from his back and massage his aching bones until they relaxed.

Tam's daydreaming stopped abruptly when he realised that Fred had called on Andy Young, who was fluent in English, Scots, German and French, to act as interpreter for himself and Gunther because, for all his poise, Gunther could speak no English and Fred had no understanding of German.

"Our glorious Field Marshal Erwin Rommel has instructed me to advise you men," Gunther explained through Andy, "that you are now all prisoners of war. You will be treated by us in accordance with the Geneva Convention. Along with all our other prisoners you will be taken by truck to Scramen and then you will march to Amstelveen. He also hopes your detention won't be long."

"March to Amstelveen?" exclaimed Fred. "But that's over a hundred miles away."

Andy nodded. "Aye, it's about two-hundred and fifty kilometres in foreign money. So everyone better make sure they've all got their heavy boots on – and that's every man amongst us!"

"And where to, after that?" came an anxious chorus.

Andy spoke to Gunther again before answering, "He says he's been told we'll then be taken by barge to Wesseling . . ."

"Where in Hell's name is Wesseling?" demanded Tam.

"Somewhere in Germany," explained Andy, who went on to add that from there they would then go some three hundred kilometres by truck and train to their POW camp, Stalag XX1B, somewhere in Poland. What he didn't know was that their journey would take them two months, mostly being frog-marched in the sweltering summer heat with little food and water. Even when they were transported by truck and train they would be so tightly crammed that it would be impossible to lie down. He was just about to tell them that he'd been told that during the march people might try to give them food and water but that if anyone did accept such things they would be shot.

There would have been a vehement response to this declaration had it not been for a sudden volley of rifle fire that rang out from the cornfield and was obviously aimed at the German soldiers. Everyone dived to the ground, while Gunther snapped his fingers and, without uttering a word, signalled with his right arm to a vehicle at the back, which resulted in a truck reversing towards the field. Once in position, its tarpaulin was raised and a machine gun was menacingly revealed. "Naw, naw!" yelled Fred, rolling across the ground and grabbing Gunther's arm. "They're just scared bairns. Let me talk to them."

Gunther, quite unmoved, brushed Fred's hand away and again raised his right hand. A second later he dropped it sharply and the cornfield was sprayed by a hail of bullets.

The fusillade seemed to go on for ever. When it finally ceased, all that could be heard were a few pitiful moans from the field. Gunther and Fred were the first to stand up and, with Andy's help to translate, Fred begged to be allowed to go and rescue the wounded.

By now, the howls of rage that were being screamed by the British prisoners at their captors resulted in them being forced at gunpoint against the wall; and all that Fred could do was to yell frantically: "For heaven's sake, will you all just *shut up*!" Once order was restored, he turned to Andy, asking him to intercede yet again with the officer. Eventually Gunther was persuaded that the ambush from the cornfield had nothing to do with the men who were lined up at the wall, but were simply fellow-Britons hoping against hope to save them. After pondering for what seemed an eternity he reluctantly agreed that Fred might go into the field. Only three of the eight lads who had run into the field were still alive. Two were unscathed and the other, a handsome eighteen-year-old, was near to death. Fred cradled him in his arms until he breathed his last.

Speaking through Andy once more, Fred persuaded Gunther to allow the two unwounded men to join with the group rather than have them shot. Fred eagerly agreed to take full responsibility for their future behaviour; otherwise they would be summarily executed – as indeed would Fred himself!

The verbal contract was finally sealed with the two men formally saluting one another. Then the distant roar of a motorbike approaching at speed drew everyone's gaze towards the far end of the village. There they spied the errant Billy Morrison whooping and waving his rifle wildly towards them.

"Billy, Billy! Get off that bleeding bike, you blasted idiot. Throw doon your rifle and get over here," screamed Fred – as did all the men.

The chorus of frantic pleas from his buddies, who couldn't bear to see another young man needlessly shot, resulted in Billy braking so fiercely that he catapulted himself over the handlebars, his rifle flying through the air before coming to rest at the feet of a German soldier. Fred immediately raced over, kicked the rifle out of Billy's reach, grabbed him by the collar and yanked the bewildered young man to his feet before dragging him over to Gunther, who disdainfully demanded to know where Billy had been. "Is it normal," he asked, "for British soldiers to behave in such an unruly and unacceptable fashion?" Andy smiled before explaining that Billy was much sought after by the local mademoiselles and, since both the tea ration and the bromide pills had run out, it was impossible to control Billy's philandering!

"Ja, Ja," chortled Gunther before adding, "We, the victorious and superior German army, acknowledge your resilience in defeat." He then raised his hand once more, saluted Fred, clicked his heels, and climbed aboard his vehicle.

Stretching to his full height, the sergeant turned to Andy and snorted, "Now, this is no for translation, see? But for all who understand the King's English, I'm saying that it's only the bloody opening skirmish they've won – no the whole bloody war!"

In later days, Fred would always admit that they were fortunate to have met such an honourable and professional soldier as the German lieutenant, Gunther Wengler – others would prove to be far less principled.

3

"So this is what they ca' a prisoner o' war camp," Tam observed. "Looks mair like a broken doon refugee ghetto to me."

"Right, lads. You'll be housed in the five huts in front of us and you'll then be allocated a bunk. And once you've settled in, you must fill in your details on pieces of paper." Fred now brandished a small notebook in his right hand.

"Why? So the Jerries can use oor details for propaganda?" challenged Billy.

"No, son. It's the Red Cross that wants them so they can notify your families that you're a prisoner of war but safe."

Tam shifted nervously from foot to foot before leading Eddie, Andy, George and Billy towards the nearest hut. Once inside, they sank down wearily on their bunks. The seemingly interminable marches, where only the minimum of food was supplied, had taken their toll. Tam remembered how they had each been given four slices of bread and a lump of cheese before they set out on the first march. Being ravenous, they devoured the food immediately. What they hadn't realised was that the march would last three days and no more food would be provided during that period. Looking at each other they realised they were all at least two stones lighter as a result of their starvation diet on the journey and that the eating of buttercups, daisies and nettles hadn't really helped. Some glanced down at the army boots that they had kept so highly polished as recruits and which were now completely worn through. They had lost so much on the long trek to this POW camp, some even their lives, and all now accepted that their precious freedom was lost for the time being. Tam's thoughts, as usual, travelled back to home. How was his wife coping, his Dinah who leant so heavily on him and who always seemed to be in need of entertainment? He remembered the last dance, in the YMCA hall at the corner of Restalrig Crescent, just before he left. Dinah of course had to be up on the floor for every dance. She was in her element with the Paul Jones dances, having a different partner every few minutes and all of them under her spell as they not only admired her grace and expertise in dancing but loved the way her blonde hair was swept up at the sides and imprisoned in tortoiseshell combs – not to mention the intoxicating smell of her Mischief perfume. Sighing, he acknowledged to himself that Dinah would survive, no matter what – but then he wondered how his bairns would cope, especially Phyllis.

Reaching into his top pocket for a notebook and pencil, Andy began to write out his personal details. That put an end to Tam's musings, especially when Andy passed the book to Eddie who then added his information. All too soon they had all written in the book except for Tam, who made no attempt to do so but simply stared long and hard at the meagre pages. No one spoke, but Andy went over and sat down beside him. "You illiterate, Tam?" he asked quietly.

Tam jumped up and shouted, "No, I'm no! My mither and faither mightnae hae been churched but they *were* married – in the registry office – ye ken, the one in Fire Brigade Street in Leith."

Shaking his head, Andy stood up. "I know you're no a

27

bastard. What I was wondering was if you could read and write."

A deep flush crept up Tam's neck and face before he nodded his head in abject embarrassment. "So I cannae read or write. So what? I'm the best shipwright – that's a carpenter ye ken – that Henry Robb's ever had."

"Okay. I'm sorry. But listen. I might have only been there a year but I'm the best English teacher David Kilpatrick's ever had. So, as we're going to be marooned here with precious little to do, how about I teach you to read and write, while you teach me how to hammer a nail in straight?"

Tam let a few minutes pass while he pondered on how he could explain to Andy, who was so brainy, that from five to seven years old he'd had one infectious disease after another and so missed the first two years of his schooling. And when he did get to school, he was put into the juniors where the teachers considered him an idiot because he could neither read nor write. This assumption resulted in him being labelled a lost cause and he was largely left to his own devices. Tam now reluctantly acknowledged that his teachers' inability to help him adequately might have been due more to the fact that there were fifty other bairns in his class than to the staff not bothering! Finally, he gave Andy a slow nod to confirm that he wished to be taught.

"Good," said Andy, relieving Tam of the notebook. "But in the meantime I'll fill in your details."

"Naw," was Tam's emphatic reply as he stretched out his neck, "I'll fill them oot mysel' once you've got me writing."

Andy nodded, but Fred, who had just come into the bunk-house, warned, "That's fine, son. But the folks back hame will be told you're missing . . . presumed . . . is that fair?"

"Maybe no. But isn't that all the more reason for Andy to get a move on wi' his teaching me?"

By the end of two months, with the help of the only book available to the prisoners – Andy's precious Holy Bible – and a dusty floor that acted both as blackboard and exercise book for writing on with a sharpened stick, Tam, whom Andy judged to be well above average intelligence, was reading and writing well enough for him to put pen to paper and now his details were on their way to the Red Cross.

The lack of writing material, however, was not the only concern for the group. Their rations appeared to grow less and less by the day and the men were becoming increasingly despondent. Fred did his best to keep their spirits up with exercise, quizzes, football and choir practices but as time passed it became ever harder. Andy, being the academic of the group, realised that if they stayed on this starvation diet they might all suffer serious consequences. He therefore suggested to Fred that he speak to the prison commandant and request a better diet – or at least more of the poor one!

Fred sensed that the commandant had been expecting him because he immediately insisted that more food would be made available if the men were willing to work in the factories situated just outside the camp. This proposal, as had already been explained to the commandant, was totally unacceptable to Fred. No way could he ask his men, nor would they consent, to assist the Germans to win the war. The commandant smiled. "No, I am no longer asking you to work in munitions. What I'm offering now is more food, including some meat, if your men will take up work in the sugar-beet factory."

Fred hesitated. He had brought his men thus far with the loss of only four. If they could not have more food, then disease, especially dysentery, would soon take hold. He therefore solemnly advised the commandant that, since his men were British, they valued democracy – which meant he could not give a decision on the proposal until he had consulted his men and a vote had been taken.

Fred spoke first to Andy about the trade-off and both agreed that most of the men were still in their formative years and it was vital they be kept as healthy as possible . . . even if it did mean working for the Germans. Having explained their reasoning to all concerned, Fred and Andy both hoped for an affirmative response but none was forthcoming. The men were outraged and the majority refused point-blank to have anything to do with the proposal and even likened it to the bribe given to Judas! After a few minutes, however, Billy amused everyone by asking whether there would be any young lassies working in the factory, because if so he personally would be happy to give it a go. Fred shook his head. Undernourished as he was, Billy was still prepared to chase any skirt he could find. Billy's wishful thinking seemed to give Charlie's confidence a much-needed boost and he surprised everyone by asking if there might be any way of smuggling some of the sugar beet back to camp. A short silence followed before Tam replied, "Well for a bloke like me, who was trained in Henry Robb's shipbuilding yard back in Leith, a bit o' smuggling wouldnae be a problem!"

Fred began to feel relief seeping into him as he realised the mood was gradually changing but, before he could take a vote, Andy asked why on earth they should risk their lives by stealing some of the sugar beet. And he was astounded when the chorus went up, "Moonshine! Moonshine!"

They were only into their third week of working at the factory when the moonshining came into full operation and the immature alcohol was being flung over their throats with gay abandon on Saturday nights. As soon as the liquid hit their stomachs it exploded like a fire bomb and gratifying intoxication lit up their bleak world. Their lives were also enriched by the acquisition of a dilapidated wind-up gramophone and a single record of 'Don't Sit Under The Apple Tree', by the Inkspots, which had been secured from the guards in exchange for a flagon of the moonshine! The music, although not in strict tempo, was adequate for any dance – whether tango, quick step or waltz. The exhilarating rhythm seemed to capture the inebriated souls of men who were expert in ballroom dancing. They would eagerly ask any comrade who couldn't dance, "Are you dancing?" and every reply was, "If you're asking, then I'm dancing."

There were no apparent inhibitions in this deviation from normality and each man felt that by the time he was released he'd be expert enough to show Victor Silvester how to do that slow, slow, quick, quick, slow routine with absolute mastery! When those Saturday nights were over, the men would throw themselves down on their bunks and let their yearning thoughts turn to home and their loved ones.

Tam naturally wondered how Dinah was coping and whether she was looking after his five bairns properly. Eddie thought of Betty and wondered if in the recent letter she had sent she was trying to hint that she too had been called up. All she said was, "I've changed my job. No longer in the printers. In my new job I have to wear a smart blue costume!"

And Billy, for all his philandering, would fall asleep wondering if his sweetheart, bonnie Violet Mackay, would still be keeping herself for him. Of all the women he had wooed she had been the only one not to surrender her virginity to him. He snuggled into his blanket while he recalled her saying, as she pushed him gently aside, "No, Billy. Not until our wedding night!"

4

Trying to make herself a little more comfortable by wriggling on the palliasse, Senga felt as if she'd been conned. She had been assured that life in the country would be just like it was in the films. Nice people. Good food. Plenty of fresh air and rest. And she could even expect to be dancing along the yellow brick road like Dorothy in *The Wizard of Oz*. But now, one week into her ordeal, as she saw it, evacuation was just another name for slavery! Johnny, candle in one hand, was climbing up into the hay loft and loudly asking her and Tess if they were asleep.

"Asleep?" Senga sniffed, while trying to hold back the tears. "Sleep is what I do in class and now they think I should see a nurse or doctor to see if I'm consumptive or have sleeping sickness!"

Tess rolled over from her palliasse beside Senga, leant over and gently stroked her hair. "There, there, bairn," she urged, "I think I might have got a message out to Granny Kelly asking her to come and rescue us!"

"You did?" exclaimed Johnny as he flung himself down beside his sisters. "That's just great. How on earth did ye dae it?"

"Well, d'you mind how Sheila Thompson's mammy was asked to take her home on account of her having impetigo and no one willing to take her in?" Johnny and Senga both nodded. "Well, I asked her to take a letter to Granny Kelly."

"Where did ye get the paper?"

"Och, Johnny, where d'ye think I got it?" Tess smirked. "Tore it out of my exercise book, didn't I. Anyway, back to Sheila. She did promise to take the letter to Granny but she said she didn't ken when she'd be able to get it to her."

"Hope it's right away," observed Johnny. "And look here, Tess. Did you put in the letter hoo I've to get up at half past five in the morning and feed the pigs and then clean out their sty afore I go to school?"

Tess looked askance at Johnny. "No, Johnny, I didnae. Same as I didnae say Senga and I were up at the same time and I had to milk and feed the cows before going off to school and that Senga had to look after the hens."

"But Tess," girned Senga, "if you didn't tell her that and about us being made to sleep in the barn because the farmer's wife says aw us bairns that come from Leith are lousy . . ." Senga hesitated as she thought of everything else she wanted to tell her Granny and then blurted out, "And also that we're being fed worse than the pigs . . ."

"Fed *much* worse! We've had nothing but porridge since we came here. Hot porridge, mind you, in the morning but freezing cold porridge for our tea," Johnny lamented.

"Look, all I could say in the letter was for Granny to come and rescue us and to bring the cruelty man with her."

"But why just that?" complained Senga.

"Because that's enough, especially as we've been told to watch what we say and not give the Germans any important information – you know, *careless talk costs lives*! Besides, the idea of anybody being cruel to us will sure be enough to have Granny rushing here and then we'll see if that blooming farmer can scare the living daylights out of her, the way he does us."

* * *

34

Patsy was standing on a chair slapping another coat of gun-metal blue paint on the lobby walls of 6 West Cromwell Street. Nothing, not even this dishonestly acquired paint from the shipbuilding yards, seemed to deter the bugs that frequented the stair nowadays. Patsy honestly believed that this ever-increasing plague was another way of Germany attempting to sap the resilience of the folks in Leith!

She had just bent down once more to dip her brush in the two-pound syrup tin that housed the paint when she became aware that someone was coming into the stair. "Oh, it's yourself, Etta. Slumming?"

Giving an involuntary shudder, Etta stared at the condemned building and the only thing that helped mask her disgust was the urgent news she had to impart. "Patsy," she began hesitantly. "Listen. You've got to come. Dinah needs you. I just couldn't get her calmed."

Patsy's hand flew to her mouth. "No Tam, is it?"

Etta nodded. "Telegram hasn't exactly said he's been killed – but it does say he's missing and – well, as you know, that usually means – at least *presumed* . . ."

Patsy scratched her head. "Oh Gawd, he's the only one I know that would put up wi' my Dinah. Good grief! You ken what this means?" Etta shook her head. "Just that I'm gonnae be left wi' her. Isn't life one blinking boo-row?" Whenever Patsy said "boo-row" she really meant "bugger". Etta understood and nodded.

A long silence followed, while the two women just stared at the walls, the floor, the ceiling – anywhere but at each other. Finally, Patsy said, "I'll get my coat. Oh I'm forgetting I'll hae to tell poor Mary . . . Och for sure, nae mother should lose her bairn. Against nature, that is!"

The women had just left the stair when a young girl raced up to them and asked, "D'ye ken where Mrs Kelly bides?"

"I'm Mrs Kelly," said Patsy and was surprised when the lassie pushed a note into her hand before starting to flee back the way she'd come.

"Remember," the lassie hollered back. "It wasnae me that gied you that letter!"

Patsy unscrewed the paper and read Tess's heartfelt plea. "Well," she said to herself, "you bairnies'll just need to bide and thole it the noo. Your mother and your Granny Glass are the first priorities!"

Another three long wearisome weeks had passed since Tess asked her pal to deliver the letter to her granny. On their fourth Saturday afternoon in captivity (as they saw it) the children were wondering what they could do next, as it seemed evident that either Granny Kelly never got the letter or else she didn't believe they needed rescuing. Running away and trying to walk back home had become their favoured solution and they were busily working out how best to do this, while the rain came pelting down the barn roof, when the door was suddenly flung open. The three children huddled together, thinking they were about to be summoned to do some more back-breaking work, when a familiar and beloved voice called out, "You in here, Tess, Johnny, Senga?"

The children all shouted, "Goody, goody! It's Granny," and they all began to scramble quickly down from the loft.

"So it's true you're being kept like pigs?"

Johnny nodded as he took his granny by the arm and guided her over to the ladder, but Patsy only climbed enough of the steps to let her see into the loft where the three palliasses and the three worn blankets were lying side by side. Angrily, she descended and gathered her three grandchildren into her arms. As she rocked them to and fro they were quite shocked to hear her mutter, "Bastards! Bloody bastards!"

Releasing the three children at length, Patsy told them to go and collect their things. "Everything?" asked Senga, with growing excitement.

"Everything. Not another minute do you spend here. And once you've packed everything, meet me outside."

Tess's eyes popped when she emerged into the daylight to see that her granny was walking into the farmer's house, accompanied by a police sergeant. Signalling to Senga and Johnny to follow, she quickly made her way over to the window, where the three children had a grandstand view of the kitchen and the outcome of Granny's meeting with the farmer and his wife.

"What do you mean by treating my grandchildren no better than hogs?"

The farmer's wife tried to put the table between herself and the irate Patsy. "We've treated them well," she replied defensively.

"Well?" screeched Patsy. "You call having them sleep in a barn with the animals treating them *well*?"

"There was nothing else we could do. I've my own two children to protect and, as everyone knows, children from Leith are all crawling with lice and . . ."

The farmer's wife never finished her sentence as Patsy had jumped over the top of the table and, in mid-air, had punched the woman heavily in the face. "My bairns do *not* have lice and if they have them now they got them from you. And what's this?" Patsy was now looking down, not at the blood oozing from the woman's nose, but at the three plates of cold porridge which she suspected was destined to be her grandchildren's tea.

"We sometimes put it by the fire to give it a heat for them but it's too warm for a fire the day," wheedled the farmer, who was the next victim to get a punch from Patsy.

The police sergeant now realised he had to restrain Patsy so he grabbed her firmly by the waist, which resulted in all three children charging into the kitchen to rescue their granny, while the farmer, emboldened by the sergeant's action, demanded that Patsy be charged with assault. This announcement had a calming effect on Patsy, who had no wish to spend a night in the cells. Accordingly, she looked imploringly at the sergeant who she felt was a decent man.

"Right," ordered the sergeant, making sure he rolled the "r" "If we proceed with an assault charge then this lady will have the right to say why she . . . *justifiably* . . . lost her temper." The farmer shifted uneasily. "And the whole story of the deplorable conditions these children have endured will come out." Patsy nodded. "So," and the sergeant now turned Patsy round to face him, "I think that, since you want to take them home with you the day, we should all forget what has happened here."

The farmer and his wife quickly nodded in agreement.

"But," continued the sergeant, "I consider it only right that compensation be paid for the appalling behaviour."

"Naw, naw. Just let them go. We don't want anything from them," the farmer emphasised as he began ushering Patsy and the children towards the door.

"I should hope not," replied the indignant sergeant. "It's *you* who has to compensate *them*!"

"But how could I do that?" spluttered the farmer. "I'm a poor man."

"That's right," his wife butted in. "We've not got much."

"Oh I wasn't thinking of money. Now, let's see. How about all the eggs the wee lassie had to collect for you? I think, so I do, that it would be only proper for you to give her a dozen to take home!" The farmer gave a nod of assent and promptly went to fetch the eggs – but not before the sergeant added, "And of course I'll need half a dozen for myself as some recompense for all the trouble I've gone to today to keep you out of hot water!"

The bus journey home from Lasswade seemed endless. The children were so excited and longed to see their mother again. Tess was the first to ask if there was any word of her father and Patsy said, "No-o-o."

"You sure?" Johnny insisted.

Patsy just nodded silently and was grateful when Senga began to ask about Phyllis. "Och, she's doing well enough. A wee bit weaker. But still holding on," she added quickly, diverting any other questions about Tam. She knew she would have to tell the children eventually, but at least she could put it off until they got home. She hoped desperately that the children would not be as upset as Dinah had been. Well before she had reached the Restalrig Circus house she could hear Dinah's hysterical screams and sobs. She had tried to quieten her for the sake of Phyllis, who lay imprisoned in her bed making no attempt to wipe the large tears that dropped silently from her eyes. Patsy had just managed to console Dinah when Tam's mother, Mary Glass, arrived. Mary's calm and resolute conviction that she would never believe her Tam was dead until they had found his body had astounded Patsy. Mary was so emphatic. Not a tear – just a quiet statement: "No. I'd know in here," she said, patting her breast, "if anything bad had happened to my Tam. I just know, and don't ask me why, but I do know he's still . . ."

"Alive, Granny?"

"Aye, alive, Phyllis. Alive!" Mary emphasised, wiping the tears away from Phyllis's cheek with her bare hand before kissing the girl fiercely on the forehead.

Dinah persisted however. "My life's over now. Wi' Tam gone, I'd enter a nunnery if it wasn't for the bairns." Patsy nodded but wondered what the poor nuns had done to deserve that!

On reaching Restalrig Circus, Johnny was the first of the children to burst into the house. "Johnny!" Etta whooped, leaping up from her seat by the fire to hug him.

However, when Patsy came into the room, tugging a very tired Senga by the hand, things didn't go quite as planned. "Where's Dinah?" she asked, her eyes roving around the room.

Etta shrugged. "Oh, Patsy. Her pal Eva came in and suggested, just to cheer her up, that they go up to the Palais in Fountainbridge."

"She's away to the Palais dance hall and her man no cold in his grave?" screeched Patsy, before clamping her hand to her mouth in a vain attempt to take back the words.

By now, Tess and Johnny had surrounded Patsy. "What d'ye mean . . . saying our Dad's not cold in his grave?" sobbed Tess.

"Well. Maybe he's no," Etta countered, in an effort to calm them all.

"That's right," agreed Patsy, who tried to catch hold of

Tess but was angrily rebuffed. "You see, all the telegram said was that he was missing – and that usually means . . ."

"Presumed deid!" screamed Johnny. "I hate this bloody war. Us being treated like pigs and now Daddy being . . ."

Silence fell in the room and no one noticed that Senga had slipped into the small bedroom and was now crying uncontrollably into a pillow.

5

Mary Glass had just turned into Restalrig Circus when her ears were assailed by the sound of loud shrieks emanating from her daughter-in-law, Dinah, who was hurling verbal abuse at her mother Patsy. In addition to this, a radio was being played at full blast in the background. Thinking that the screams might be the result of disastrous news from the front about her son, Tam, Mary began to race towards the house. Once up the path, she noticed the living room windows were wide open and so, instead of going to the door, she stuck her head in at the first window and called out, "Is this a private war or can anyone join in?"

"Och, it's yourself, Mary," Patsy responded. "Come away in and see if you can make this daft lassie of mine see some sense."

Much to Patsy's astonishment, Mary made no attempt to withdraw her head. Instead, she simply pushed her body further in until she finally landed on all fours on the floor. "Noo, what's this aw aboot?" demanded Mary, as she stood up and skipped over to kiss Phyllis.

"It's me," yelled Dinah, "telling this . . . this interfering mother o' mine that just because the Jerries are knocking hell out o' London that's no reason for my bairns to be sold back into slavery!"

"Slavery?" queried Mary in some puzzlement.

"They've been given the chance to be evacuated to a country estate where they'll be safe and well looked after,"

Patsy explained, lifting a letter from the mantelpiece and handing it to Mary.

"Look, Mammy, the pasting everybody said we would get here hasnae happened, has it?"

"That right? And what was the first place the Luftwaffe hit when this blinking war started?"

Dinah laughed derisively before quipping, "Oot there in the Forth. And a right shambles that was. For two years we'd aw been practising on how, when the siren went, we were to get oursels into the Anderson shelters while putting on our gas masks. And when the raid did happen, the dopey air-raid wardens forgot to sound the alarm."

Mary bristled. "You blaming my Archie's section, Dinah? It wasnae their fault that they planes came at two-thirty in the afternoon." She now turned to Patsy. "As Gawd's ma judge, Patsy, I'll never forget yon day. Oh aye, the efternoon o' sixteenth October 1939 will bide in my mind for ever!"

"Right enough. We weren't expecting them afore supper time. Bloody cheek they had, turning up just when the bairns had been let oot o' school."

"Dinah," shouted Patsy, "that's quite enough! Mary here has enough to contend with – I mean – Tam being missing, poor Archie having to do his bit here wi' some other air-raid wardens – that dinnae seem to be up to their job – and Dod ..." She didn't continue as she knew Mary was ashamed of Dod, her third son. She did say to people now that he had deliberately got himself into prison because he was a conscientious objector but in truth he was a problem child, having been sent to Borstal for thuggery when he was just twelve years old. The only thing of value he got out of that Borstal training was an ability to play the trumpet exceptionally well. Such a pity it was that, when the police arrived two years ago to arrest him for black-marketeering, instead of blowing his trumpet he banged it over the arresting officer's head while pushing some contraband butter up his nose!

"You know, Patsy! It wasnae the fault o' Archie and his mates that 602 and 603 squadrons thought it was just another practice. I mean, how can they be blamed because the Brylcreem Boys were sitting on their arses at East Fortune and Turnhouse playing poker while the Jerries were knocking hell out o' our ships in the Forth?" argued Mary, who was anxious that all the blame for the fiasco didn't fall on her least able son.

It was now time for Dinah's ten-year-old Johnny to provide a display and he startled everyone by giving a loud demonstration of a ducking and diving aeroplane. "Aye, but once oor flying ace, Patrick Gifford, knew what was happening he and his pals got their Hurricanes airborne with the guns goin, 'Ack! Ack!' And they didnae half put the frighteners on they Jerries. Shot two o' them down and sent the others tearing back to Germany, so they did."

Patsy nodded in assent. "Looking for our braw battleship, the *HMS Hood*, they were. Good thing she wasn't there. Mind you, I think when they couldn't find her they knocked hell out of all the other ships just for spite."

"And then the damaged German planes flew so low, they did, trying to get back hame," interjected Mary, ignoring Patsy's observations, "that the bairns in the street could see the swastikas on their wings and helmets. Know Ivy Dickson?" All nodded towards Mary. "Well, she says the plane that was coming down on Restalrig Crescent was losing height so fast you could smell the soorkraut the pilot had had for his denner the night afore."

Dinah rolled her eyes and looked up at the ceiling before commenting: "Mind you, you've got to hand it to the blooming Joppa Christians, who you'll remember gave the two pilots a proper military send-off after fishing them oot o' the sea at Port Seton."

"Right enough. They good folk," enthused Patsy, "let them lie in yon St Philip's church the night afore their burial at Portobello cemetery, so they did. I think they did that because they'd spared the bairns. Could have killed some o' them, so they could." Patsy looked about the room before continuing in a whisper, "Mind you, that wasn't reported in the news – censored oot it was because they didnae want people thinking there might be some good Germans."

"Right enough, but what about our sixteen brave sailor laddies that were killed when their ships were bombed by your pals – no to mention the forty they hospitalised. What did the Christians do for them?"

"Look here, Dinah, I ken what you're trying to do by going on about the Germans – avoiding the real issue here the day," Patsy emphasised. "So let me tell you that the bairns *are* going to be evacuated."

"But why has that to be, Mammy?"

"Because in the first raid there were no civilian casualties but the second one in August last year when the mine was dropped in Leith . . ."

"When we forgot to sound the sirens yet again. But then that time did they no come when we were haeing our tea and no our supper?" mocked Dinah.

"Okay. But there *were* civilian casualties that time." Patsy shook her head. "Still think o' that wee laddie delivering his night papers in Largo Place – blown to smithereens he was and that's the reason your bairns are off next week to

45

Linlithgow. And before you start, that's what their faither wanted – wanted them safe."

"All of them?" Mary asked, gazing at her five grandchildren.

"Well, naturally no Phyllis; and I'm letting Tess stay to help with her. So only Johnny, Senga and Elsie will go."

"*You're* letting Tess stay? Big deal!" jeered Dinah. "Whose bairns are they, yours or mine?"

"Your Mammy's quite right, Dinah," said Mary. "My Tam did want them evacuated. Dead scared he was for them after the first raid. And I always wonder if he knew about the one in August last year? Just said that the Jerries had carried out a raid somewhere in the East of Scotland – but since the mine that was dropped blew parts o' Leith to smithereens we knew it was us."

"So you think Tam's still alive do you, Mary?" asked Patsy, shaking her head.

"I *know* he is."

"You do?" Dinah exclaimed. "How?"

"Well, last week did I no go doon to a séance at the Spiritualist Church in Bath Street at Portobello?"

"Are you saying he got a message through to you from the spirit world?"

"No, Patsy," said Mary with a shake of the head. "I didnae get a message and that's how I ken he's still alive." Dinah and Patsy looked askance while Mary continued, "Honestly, the medium was awfy guid, so she was. Explained to me, she did, that you can only get a message through if the person you want a message from is really in the spirit world!"

* * *

"Right, missus," the conductress called out as the driver brought the bus to a shuddering halt.

"Oh, is this it?" asked Patsy, signalling to the children to get up, gather up their luggage and follow her off the bus.

Once everyone was safely out, the conductress leant over and pointed to the old stone bridge over the Union Canal. "Just cross over the bridge there and follow the road. First you'll come to the wee Home Farm, and then," she hesitated, looked at little Elsie before adding, "it's a good stretch of the legs till you come to the Big Hoose. Cannae miss it. Naw, you just cannae miss it."

Patsy nodded her thanks before she and her three grandchildren, Johnny, Senga and Elsie, began their trek to Andrew Craig's ancestral home.

They had trudged for twenty minutes before the house loomed into view. Patsy was so awestruck by its size and splendour that she dropped Elsie, to whom she had been giving a colly-buckie. "You'll need to walk by yourself from here," she whispered.

"But why?" moaned Elsie, who was very small and delicate for her years.

"Because you don't want the folk to think you're a baby."

"But, Granny, she *is* just a baby," Senga emphasised.

Patsy shook her head, grabbed Elsie's hand and began dragging her towards the house. The nearer they came to the building, the more Patsy thought the most remarkable thing about it, apart from its size, was the large and intimidating metal-studded wooden door which stood ajar, as if to offer a somewhat intimidating welcome.

Johnny had just raised his hand to bang on the knocker when the inner half-glazed door opened and a smiling woman, possibly in her mid-thirties, came forward with an outstretched hand to Patsy. "I'm Mrs Stoddard, one of the two teachers here. And you must be Mrs Glass."

This introduction only added to Patsy's bewilderment and the children were greatly amused to see their granny give a small curtsey before replying, "No, I'm Mrs Kelly. The bairns' grandmother, your ladyship. Dinah, my daughter, the bairns' mother, had to stay and look after our Phyllis – she cannae be left alone – she cannae walk, you see."

Nodding, and signalling for the family to follow, Mrs Stoddard turned and led them into the large reception hall where children's coats, shoes and Wellingtons were housed. "This is where you children will hang your coats," she said, pointing to the coat-stands. "And underneath there is plenty of room for your outdoor footwear. So let's get that done," she said briskly, helping Elsie out of her coat and hanging it on a hook for her because Elsie was too small to reach it.

Senga wanted to explain that they only ever had one pair of shoes at a time, so there was no need to take them off, but she gulped, remembering that on the list of what they should take was a pair of slippers. Quickly, she fished these out and slid them on.

Mrs Stoddard then opened another large, imposing door and the children gawped on entering an enormous drawing-room bathed in the late morning sun that was shining through the long sparkling windows. It was true that it was now being used as the school room but even the blackboard, desks and chairs could not diminish its elegance. A huge marble fireplace, complete with brass-handled poker and tongs alongside a scuttle filled with logs, took up the whole length of the nearest wall, while the grand piano had been moved up against the far wall – everything here reminded you that this house had been the home of 'oor betters', as Granny Glass would say.

Looking directly at Patsy, Mrs Stoddard smiled before saying, "I'll take the children through to the dining hall. They've come just in time for lunch and before you leave us, Mrs Kelly, I'll just go over some of our house rules with you. When you have twenty-one children in a house, you must have rules." She pointed to a high-backed wooden chair for Patsy to sit on until she came back, while saying to the children, "Come on now, say goodbye to your grandmother."

For Johnny, Senga and Elsie, their first day at the Craigs (as all the children living there called it) proved quite a daunting experience. They had been made to feel very welcome, not only by the staff but by the other children, who it seemed came from all parts of the country. Four of the evacuees didn't even seem to mind that they never had visitors on a Sunday because they knew their parents were doing vital war duties far, far away from Linlithgow.

The dormitories were situated on the third floor and once Senga and Elsie realised they were expected to sleep alone in single beds they both became tearful. It wasn't that the beds weren't comfortable or warm – it was just the thought of waking up in the night and not having the comfort of another human being lying next to you.

To help cope with the solitude, Senga first wrapped her blanket tightly round herself and curled herself into a ball. Then she clasped her hands before imprisoning them between her knees. To her surprise, sleep overtook her very quickly but she woke suddenly around midnight when she felt a tugging at her blanket. Rolling over and disentangling herself from the bedclothes, she was surprised to see Elsie standing by the bed and trembling.

"Senga, I'm feart. Really feart – and my teddy disnae like it here either. Could we no get intae bed beside you?"

Senga nodded. Quickly opening up the blanket to let Elsie climb in beside her, the pair were soon snuggled safely together, just as they would have been at home.

Dinah and her friend Etta inhaled slowly on their second cigarette. "Oh, are these no just sheer heaven, Etta, are they no?"

"And you got a whole tin o' them." Etta picked up the can to inspect it and noted it was navy issue, marked, "Fifty Capstan Navy Strength Cigarettes". "And how did you come by them?"

"Got them off a sailor."

"Did he come on your bus like?"

"Naw. Naw. I met him in the servicemen's canteen up the East End o' Princes Street."

Etta nodded before taking another cigarette from the tin. "Good we've got Phyllis bedded down for the night and it'll be a wee while afore Tess gets back from the pictures." She paused and gave a slight cough as the smoke haze surrounded the two women. "But, ken something? I find it awfy quiet without aw the others."

"Aye, oor blessed Saint Patsy, saviour of my bairns as she sees herself, should be back ony time now from Linlithgow. Look, afore the auld battleaxe gets in, how about you and me having a bit toasted cheese and a cup of tea wi' twa sugars!"

The mention of toasted cheese had a bad effect on Etta and she started to boak. "You still throwing up?" Dinah asked, screwing up her face in disgust. Etta nodded. "Must be something wrang wi' ye . . ."

Etta lifted the poker and began stirring the last embers of the fire back into life. "Dinah," she said slowly without looking up. "The one good point your mammy says you have is . . ." Etta hesitated before whispering, ". . . is that you can keep a secret."

"Oh, Etta, ye're . . . no? But here ye are. I mean are ye *really* saying . . . you're on the road?" stammered Dinah as she bent over and rubbed Etta's knee.

Etta nodded.

"You mean you've actually missed? How long?"

"Three weeks."

"Och, is that no just wonderful? And it's what you've always wanted. See when you get over the morning sickness you'll feel just great."

Etta continued to poke the fire while sighing deeply.

"And how does Harry feel about it? Bet he's cock-a-hoop?"

Etta stopped annoying the fire and just sat staring into space as big silent tears ran down her face.

"I ken ye're getting on a fair bit for your first bairn – but you'll be fine," Dinah said reassuringly. However, when Etta slumped even further down in the chair, Dinah realised there was something far wrong. It was not as simple as Etta being worried about becoming an older mother. It was something that Dinah should be seeing. But something she wasn't seeing. Then it slowly dawned on her that she'd never seen Harry, not once, in the last six months! "Wh – wh – when was Harry last home on leave?" she spiered.

Etta shook her head, "That's the trouble . . . he's no been home."

"Oh," was all Dinah could mutter.

"Aye. Oh."

"Are you sure you're away then?"

Etta nodded. "Aye, and Harry's no going to be pleased because – he's – well he's no . . ."

"Don't mean to pry but, well – who is to blame then?"

"The Germans," blurted out Etta as sobs racked her body.

Dinah shook her head. "But we've no been invaded by the Germans. Do you no mean they randy Poles that are squatting down in the Craigentinny Army Camp?"

"No. The Germans are to blame. All four hundred of them!"

Dinah was speechless at first but when she finally managed to utter some words all she could say was, "Etta, are you saying that the fact you're expecting is down to four hundred Germans taking advantage o' you?"

"No. They didn't take advantage of me. Frightened the living daylights out of me, so they did."

"They frightened you? But getting a fright doesn't . . ." Dinah didn't continue as Etta went on to explain.

"Remember last month – the thirteenth and fourteenth of March – when all these German bombers flew over us on their way to blitz poor Clydebank to smithereens?" Dinah nodded. "Aye, well, on the first night I was asleep when the siren went and Jacob Simpson woke me up telling me to go with him to the shelter. But I heard all the din, saw all the flashes of the searchlights." Etta put her hands over her ears. "Those guns. Oh, Dinah! I was so scared that I told Jacob I just couldn't go outside and run for the shelter. So he just patted my head and said not to worry and that we'd just go back to bed . . ."

Dinah's eyes were now like saucers and her breath was coming in short pants. "You mean? No . . . you just can't . . .!" Etta made no reply but only nodded her head. "Oh. You do? Now let's get this straight. The father of your baby is – your father-in-law, Jacob?"

Etta's head had sunk so low that her chin was being pushed into her neck.

"But that's unbelievable," gasped Dinah. "Jacob was married for years and there were no children so he and his wife adopted Harry. You and Harry have been married for years and you never fell. You jump once into bed with Jacob and . . ."

"Because I was that scared," Etta retaliated fiercely, lifting her head in defiance. Then her head dropped again before she continued in a tearful and more conciliatory tone. "And I've been scared ever since!"

Dinah, who had risen to her feet, now sank down into the chair opposite Etta. Could she really believe what she was being told? Here was comfortable, untidy Etta, who always looked like a shaggy dog only wanting to be loved and needed, having an affair with her ageing father-in-law. And to add to Dinah's astonishment was the fact that Jacob, who was the chief accountant in Gibson's Shipping Company, was so stooped that he couldn't even lift his head and was devoutly religious. Her thoughts were interrupted though by Etta asking, "Dinah, what *can* I do? You're so good at getting out of pickles."

Dinah shook her head. "But this is more than a pickle. It could be grounds for divorce – maybe even justifiable *murder*!" She did concede however that Etta was not the only one to blame here – if her husband Harry had shown her only a little love and attention she wouldn't have had to seek it elsewhere. She knew this was true because that was surely the reason why her friend spent so much time looking after Phyllis.

A few minutes passed while Dinah pondered and Etta just sobbed. Eventually Dinah asked, "Are you *sure* you're only three weeks late?"

"Aye. Jacob's lonely, too, so we've been comforting each other ever since the nights of the Clydebank raids."

"Aye, well. Here was me thinking the Jerries were only trying to bomb Clydebank into submission and here's you been . . ." Dinah paused. Something truly drastic had to be done. Etta would never cope with the gossip, the sniggering and, most importantly, the cold-shouldering from the holier-than-thou scandal-mongers that would undoubtedly creep out of the woodwork. Once or twice Dinah was about to speak because she thought she had an answer – then would close her mouth and shake her head. That was, until the perfect solution struck her and she smiled triumphantly before announcing: "Look, here's what we do. You and I will go to Pitreavie tomorrow."

"Oh no, I just couldn't face Harry. Well, not right now."

"But you're gonnae do more than face him. You're gonnae tell him your mother invited us over to South Queensferry for the day and with you being only a ferry boat's sail away and you missing him so very, very much, you just had to look him up."

"And?"

"Och, do I have to spell it out for you? Somehow – and anywhere at all – you get him to some quiet spot and . . . well, you ken . . ."

Etta shook her head. "I just couldn't. I mean how could you ask me to degrade myself outside in the open air?"

"Look here," exploded Dinah, "just you imagine there are four hundred German planes flyin' right above you. That should put enough fear into you to get things sorted."

"Oh, I think I see what you're getting at, Dinah," murmured Etta, after having taken a good few minutes to consider the proposal. "But you're forgetting that my baby is due in December, no in February."

"So you'll just be like yon Carol Stone who last week had a ten pound, four month premature weakling!"

Dinah vigorously massaged the sides of her buttocks as she exclaimed, "Oh, this rickety auld bus. My poor backside."

"No bothering me," replied Patsy, looking somewhat askance at her daughter.

"Aye, and if I was as well padded as you I wouldnae be moaning either."

Patsy ignored the insult. "No be long till we're there. I'm just starving for the bairns."

"That right? And whose idea was it to send them to the God-forsaken place where the first thing they did was to volunteer for slavery?"

Patsy smiled as she recalled the three letters they'd received from the children since they had been evacuated six weeks ago.

The first letter had been from Johnny who said what a great place the Craigs was and how he had been sailing on a pond in an old tin bath. Because it was holed you had to keep bailing out and, as Elsie was just useless at that, they had nearly sunk. But even if they had gone under there was no need to worry, as the depth of the pond was not over his head – only Elsie's!

Letter number two came as a big surprise since it was from Senga. She had bragged that she was no longer a duffer because Mrs Carruthers spent time every evening helping with her reading and writing. She had learned so fast that she was now able to write – not joined-up writing yet (that would take a few days more) – but here was her first attempt at writing a note home. The letter went on to say that Johnny had gone down the back road of the estate to the farm where he'd got talking to the farmer and explained that he knew a lot about rearing pigs as he had spent one whole month in Lasswade tending the animals there and could he get a paid job looking after the farmer's pigs after school? Senga went on to say that the farmer, who didn't think a month of training with pigs was adequate, had taken quite a bit of persuasion but he did give in and Johnny was really enjoying the chore. What she couldn't put in the letter (because Mrs Carruthers was helping her with the composition of it) was that Johnny was saving up the money he earned in case they had to get home quickly if Daddy was found or whatever and that in another two weeks he should have earned enough for the bus fares home for them all! Senga went on to explain that she was now helping the land-girl, Dorothy. Dorothy had been called up to the Land Army, and even although she was kitted out in the uniform and looked the part, she didn't know everything she should about collecting eggs and Senga had offered to put her right. Senga herself wasn't being paid in money, like Johnny, but Dorothy had promised that when Granny Patsy came to visit she would be given the afternoon lay and sometimes that could be as much as ten eggs! The letter ended by saying, if there was any word of where Daddy was, could she have the address as she could then write to him. The third letter was again from Johnny. It contained a ten-shilling note with the request that a football be bought and also some sweets if there was any change left, and could it please come this Sunday.

Looking out of the bus window, Patsy smiled peacefully – but suddenly remembered that she wanted to quiz Dinah, so gave her daughter a vigorous dig in the ribs. "Here, Dinah," she said, "did you know that Etta is . . ." Patsy paused, looking warily around the bus to make sure she was not overheard before whispering, "on the road?"

"Is she? Now fancy that! And when will she be better?" Dinah replied, turning to look out of the window since she didn't want her mother to see her satisfied smile.

"Late January or early February, so she says." Patsy waited for a reaction from Dinah but as none was forthcoming, she continued, with a knowing cock of her head. "Seems Harry can't believe it either but he's coming home on his days off now. Know something?" Patsy leant forward so she could see if there would now be an obvious response from Dinah before continuing, "I think that day you got me to watch Phyllis so you and Etta could go over to South Queensferry . . . well I guess that mousy Etta had good reason to go a fair bit further."

Dinah smiled but made no reply: she knew just how far Etta had gone that day.

"Here. We're here," Patsy exclaimed as the bus shuddered to a halt. "And look! The bairns have come to the road-end to meet us."

57

6

Dinah was lovingly stroking one of the precious nylons that she had carefully laid upon her left hand.

"Well," asked Etta, as she picked up the bottle of leg make-up and shook it vigorously. "Are you going to wear them tonight or am I going to plaster your legs with this?"

"It's not the make-up I mind. It's getting the line straight. You know, no matter how hard you try to keep yon eyebrow pencils going in a straight line they just go zigzagging." Etta nodded. "So the choice is: do I go out with pencilled-on seams that look as if they've had one too many – not to mention the cold turning my flesh blue – or should I risk wearing my very first pair of precious nylons, the ones I got from that nice Canadian airman?"

"The choice is yours. But don't forget the other problem is that you'll need to jump up on the table for me to do my artistry on your pins because I just can't . . ." Etta stopped and patted her swollen belly. "No. There's no way I could bend down on the floor to help you."

"Suppose it's the pencil job then," sighed Dinah, jumping up on the table, "because I'm no wanton hussy, I simply can't go out bare-legged."

Etta had started to smooth the fake tan make-up over Dinah's legs when there came a sharp knock at the door. Both women looked at each other. Etta shook her head and held up her cream-covered hands. They looked towards Phyllis but since she obviously couldn't move there was nothing else for it but for Dinah to jump down and answer the summons.

Opening the door, she was confronted by a telegraph boy holding out an envelope.

"No," she cried. "I don't want it."

"But, missus, aren't you Mrs Thomas Glass?" Dinah nodded. "Then you *have* to take it," insisted the boy, thrusting the telegram into Dinah's hand.

"Bad news?" enquired Etta who was just emerging from the kitchen where she had gone to wash her hands.

Dinah grimaced. "Suppose it is. Suppose it's what we've all been dreading."

Etta went over to Phyllis, lifted her hand and began stroking it. "Well, open it, Dinah, and let's hear the worst."

Slowly Dinah pushed her thumb under the flap of the envelope and then withdrew the telegram. As she began to read, tears welled up in her eyes and spilled down her cheeks.

"So Tam's dead?" sniffed Etta.

Dinah shook her head. "No. He's alive. Alive, thank God! But he's a prisoner of war!"

Christmas Eve at the Craigs had an air of magic about it. A large decorated fir tree took up one corner of the schoolroom and the desks had all been pushed against a wall so that the centre of the room was bare and ready for the party to begin. Johnny was sitting on a chair with a smile on his face that would have melted an iceberg.

"You like Christmas, Johnny?" Mrs Carruthers asked. "But then you probably got some nice Christmas cards in the post today."

Johnny cackled. "Naw, Miss, we dinnae send cards."

"So you're happy because Santa Claus will be coming tonight?"

"Santa Claus? Don't you ken he's a Tory, Miss? He only gies to them that has lots and lots – never to us poor folk."

"So why are you so happy?"

Johnny took a letter addressed to himself that had arrived in the morning post. He thrust it into Mrs Carruthers' hand and she began to read from it. "Oh, this is truly good news. Your Daddy's been found in a prisoner of war camp! Oh, Johnny, that is indeed the best Christmas present you and your family could get!"

However, before Johnny could reply, a distraught Senga burst into the room and declared, "I'm no eating any Christmas dinner because I know now why we were asked to feed up Tom, Dick and Harry!"

"You can't mean they're our . . ." protested Johnny.

"They are, and not only that, but once the cook had throttled them and hauled the feathers off them, she threw them in a big witch's cauldron with some carrots, leeks and barley." Senga was now sobbing uncontrollably. "And then she said to us: 'Bet your sweet life you'll never have tasted such wonderful cock-a-leekie soup like we're going to make!'"

It fell to Etta to inform Patsy, yet again, that Dinah was away out with fake-tanned legs and possibly celebrating by drinking and dancing the night away.

"Och," was the disgusted reply from Patsy. "Do you mean to say she's just been told her man's still alive and yet she's gone out on the randan?"

Etta nodded. "But, Patsy, I think Dinah going AWOL again is the least of our worries."

"You do?"

"Aye, you see Phyllis hasnae been herself all day. Wheezing and gasping. Hasnae eaten a thing. Took me all my time to get her to have a wee drink o' water."

Both women went over to the wooden bed and gazed down at what appeared to be a peacefully sleeping child.

"Oh my Gawd," exclaimed Patsy as she bent over and lifted Phyllis in her arms. "She's away. My wee angel's away. And I never got time to say goodbye." Both women were now weeping uncontrollably.

"It must have just happened," protested Etta. "I was speaking to her just before you came in."

Patsy made no reply. She just kept rocking her grand-daughter back and forth while she lovingly stroked her face. "Knew I couldn't keep you forever," she whispered to the dead child. "But I just hoped you'd stay a wee while longer – specially now your Daddy will be coming home."

Nothing could distract Patsy from mourning the loss of her granddaughter. Neither the sound of the outside door opening when Tess returned home nor Tess's subsequent wails when Etta told her that Phyllis was dead had any effect. Only when Tess jumped back suddenly from the bed and screamed, "Oh, Etta, you dirty thing!" did Patsy become aware again of what was happening around her.

"Why are you saying that to Etta? It's not her fault that Phyllis suddenly . . ." Patsy was finding it so hard to say the word – dead! "We were warned she'd have to leave us one day and that it would happen quickly, like this," Patsy said through her sobs.

"But, Granny, I'm not blaming Etta for Phyllis. It's just that she has stood there and peed hersel'!"

Patsy glanced down at the linoleum floor that was now

awash and then raised her eyes to Etta's, waiting for some explanation, but all Etta could do was mumble, "I've no been myself the day either. The pain in my back's sheer agony now this bairn's so big."

"Oh, Etta, don't you ken you're in labour?"

"But my baby's not due till February," protested Etta, who had so many times told the lie about the time of the expected birth that she now believed it herself.

"Maybe so," replied Patsy. "But Tess, just you run down Restalrig Road to the big house the midwives bide in." Tess looked bewildered. "Ye ken, just up from the Leith Provi." Still unsure, Tess slowly nodded. "And tell them to get to Etta's as soon as they can." Patsy now looked at Etta who was visibly wincing as a long contraction gripped her and Patsy called out after Tess, "In fact, tell them sooner than soon!"

"But, Granny, will they not all be in bed?" Tess shouted back.

Sheer exasperation made Patsy yell, "Aye, but when they hear the bell it tells them a baby's on the way so they get up! So move yourself."

Turning to Etta, who was now lying on the floor, Patsy dragged her upright. "It's no that I don't want to help you but with Phyllis lying here you'd be much more comfortable at home." With that she hauled Etta to her feet, flung her coat round her shoulders and then together the two women made the slow and painful journey to Learig Close with Etta stopping frequently as yet another pain engulfed her.

They had just turned into Learig Close when Patsy realised that Rachel Campbell, returning as usual from work, was just ahead of them and she called out to her.

Immediately Rachel laid down her heavy shopping bags and ran to help Patsy. "But Etta was just saying to me yesterday that she didn't know what size she would be by February – and here, the wee soul's on its way now."

Patsy nodded before going on to explain about Phyllis and was grateful when Rachel replied emphatically, "Look, you get yourself back to the wee lassie. Sure she might be in heaven but she shouldn't be lying there all by herself. Now, off you go and I'll look after Etta. I'll call my neighbour, Peggy, to come and help me until the nurses come." Rachel stopped as Etta gave out yet another piercing scream.

It was three hours later, in the morning, when Rachel tapped gently at the Glasses' door in Restalrig Circus. Immediately it was opened by a man that Rachel thought was Patsy's husband but because of the blackout she wasn't able to see him clearly – though she could certainly recognise the smell of alcohol on his breath.

"I, er. Well, I've come . . ."

"What?" bellowed the man, swaying to and fro. "This is a hoose o' mournin', I tell ye. So if ye're on the cadge, just sling yer hook."

Rachel was about to react angrily when Patsy opened the door further. "Oh, it's yourself, Rachel. Ignore this idiot," and with that she pushed her husband Danny back. "Come away in."

"No, no," replied Rachel, shaking her head. "I just came round to tell you, with you being so friendly with Etta Simpson like, that she's had a nice wee boy."

"Oh, but with him being one or two months early, he'll be very small."

Rachel looked bewildered. "Well, he is wee, but no wee

for his age. Weighed in, he did, at nine-and-a-half pound – and, before you ask, that was without a nappy!"

Patsy pondered before asking, "And who does he take after?"

"Oh, his Granddad. Spitting image of old Mr Simpson, so he is. Even got the long accountant's fingers for counting the money."

Patsy just nodded. Evidently even on a night like this she could still put two and two thegither.

Rachel had turned to leave when a giggling woman, Patsy's daughter, approached the pathway. Patsy immediately sprang in front of Rachel, blocking her view, but she did hear Dinah being given a loud slap by her mother. Rachel then had to jump back sharply, as Patsy roughly bundled her daughter past her while shouting at Dinah's military escort to "Boo-row off!" She then went on to yell at Dinah, her voice cracking with emotion, "Where in the name of heaven have you been when you were needed here at home?"

"Dancing. Celebrating. 'Cause my Tam's safe."

Another loud slap from Patsy found its target as she retorted, "Aye, our Tam's safe and so is my Phyllis. Safe in the arms of Jesus!"

7

The constant knocking on the front door roused Patsy from her catnapping but, finding it hard to fully awaken, it took her some time to open the door.

"What do you want?" she shouted after the retreating figure.

"It's only me," Mary answered, turning round and walking back to where Patsy was standing. "Just got settled in and was fancying a wee cuppa . . . but I've nae sugar."

Patsy smiled and with a beckoning gesture invited Mary into her home. The house in Restalrig Road was where she'd moved to a year ago when Danny Kelly, her paralysed husband, was released from hospital in a wheelchair. His paralysis had stemmed from an inebriated backward fall down the well-worn stairs in West Cromwell Street. Of course, according to Danny, the blame lay with the housing factor who should have kept the stairs in a decent state of repair. He'd been vehement that the accident had nothing at all to do with his own drunken stupor. Patsy thought back to Danny and the short time he had lived in the Restalrig Road house before his death. Such a pity it was that the Learig Inn had been so handy. Indeed, most people were amazed to see how well Danny could manoeuvre his wheelchair down to the pub. And it was an even bigger pity that on leaving there one night he'd decided to steer himself into the path of a No.13 bus. But at least his end had been mercifully instantaneous.

The ground floor, left-hand house in a six-in-a-block tenement, which was situated next to the YMCA, really suited Patsy very well. It was small but the accommodation was much better than the room and kitchen in West Cromwell Street. Here, she had a living room, a couple of bedrooms, a small kitchen and a bathroom all to herself. Patsy truly regretted that she hadn't had this house when Phyllis had been alive, since that would have been so handy being just minutes away from Restalrig Circus, which meant she could have spent much more time with the bairn. And now, with Phyllis's other Granny, Mary Glass, being re-housed in Restalrig Road, in the superior flats just opposite the shops, life could have been so good for Phyllis.

Patsy went over to the sideboard, took out her sugar bowl and poured half of the contents into a cup before handing it to Mary. "That's half of what I have." Mary nodded and from her pocket took out a brown paper bag. She carefully poured the contents of the cup into it and handed the cup back to Patsy.

"Settling in?" Patsy asked, dragging a chair out from the table and sitting down.

Mary silently nodded assent while pulling out a chair to sit down on. "Aye, wasn't I just jammy bumping into Annie Forbes and her hating being in Restalrig Road and looking for an exchange back to West Cromwell Street. Cannae understand why she wasnae grateful for a lavvy aw to herself. Anyway . . ."

Patsy knew Mary all too well and realised she wanted to tell Patsy something. "Private and confidential like," she would whisper to Patsy when she was ready to confide.

"Staying long enough for a cuppa?" asked Patsy. Mary

nodded. "Well, I'll just put the kettle on. Mind you, Mary, if you're going to ladle in the sugar like you usually do, then you'll have to take it out of that lot you've just put in the brown paper poke. Fair's fair."

Patsy had just poured the tea when Mary blurted out, "Dod's getting oot the morn."

"Oh, done his time already?"

"Naw. Well . . . aye. You see, he got time off for guid behaviour."

"Good behaviour? Well, well, well." And Patsy sucked in her lips as she savoured her tea. "That's a first for him – so you must be real pleased."

Mary shook her head. "Naw. You see, when he comes oot o' Saughton the morn they'll be handing him his call-up papers afore they shut the doors ahint him!"

"Are you saying they're calling him up straight away?"

"Aye." Mary moved her head closer to Patsy. "I think the guid behaviour thing is just them taking my Dod for a hurl. I mean, they ken he doesnae knock the hell oot o' folk unless he kens them real well. I mean to say, Patsy, have you ever known him to be charged with thumping anybody he wasnae on first-name terms wi' "

Patsy took her time before answering, "But now we know for sure that we're going to win the war . . ."

"We are?" Mary replied, making no attempt to hide her incredulity.

"Of course we are! Surely you're no forgetting that, firstly, our braw Eighth Army sorted out Rommel at El Alamein in October last year and then just back there in July did the Russians no blooter all the German tanks at Kursk?"

Mary looked away. "Okay, you might be right," she said,

turning back to face Patsy. "But why, oh why then do they want my Dod?"

Patsy nodded. "That's just what I'm wondering," she said. What she didn't tell Mary was that surely the powers that be must be mad to risk everything they had gained by putting Dod on the front line! Good heavens, didn't they know he'd sell his Granny if the price was right – never mind trading any future victories?

The small home bakery in Restalrig Road was open from six o'clock in the morning selling freshly baked rolls and bran scones. Even if the shop had opened at five o'clock there would still have been a queue of eager customers. This Friday was no different. Patsy had just staggered through with a red-hot tray of rolls when the baker opened the door and the first three customers crammed themselves into the limited space. "Sleep in, Patsy?" joked Wilma Johnston.

"No," was Patsy's curt reply. "I've been in here since half past four. Ye ken! While you were still lying in your kip, I was earning my daily bread. So what's it the day? The same half-dozen rolls and two bran?"

"Aye. Here, I'm real glad your Dinah's getting herself out and about again. I thought she was never going to get over your poor wee Phyllis. And then with her dad following on so quick it seemed to knock the life clean oot o' her."

Patsy drew herself up sharp. What on earth was this woman talking about? Dinah had been a model of good behaviour since the night of Phyllis's death nearly two years ago. And not only had her behaviour been exemplary but she regularly visited the bairns in Linlithgow and wrote every week to Tam – even although there never seemed to be any letters getting out of the prisoner of war camp.

"Mind you," Wilma blundered on, "I'll bet she's fair missing yon tall, dark, handsome GI" Then, adding to Patsy's discomfiture and terror, Wilma turned to the others in the queue and licked her lips as she told them, "Sure like a film star, he was. The best-looking of the hale tribe that Dinah and her pals had in tow!"

"There's your order. Next please," Patsy hissed through gritted teeth, as she tossed the bag of hot rolls in Wilma's direction.

"Getting them for nothing, am I?" Wilma asked cheekily, while thumping the money down on the counter.

"Sorry," mumbled Patsy, grabbing the coins and tossing them into the till. "I'm no quite mysel' the day. Need three jobs I do, just to keep my head above water. And I'm that tired, I'm nearly drowning." Patsy was indeed exhausted because not only did she work five hours at the bakery every morning but three afternoons a week she cleaned for the piano teacher who owned one of the big houses down in Restalrig Road – while on Friday and Saturday nights she served in Angelo's fish and chip shop. Yet what else could she do? She had to work to keep herself and there weren't many who would employ someone of her age. Oh aye, being sixty-one had its drawbacks, one of which was to be regarded as being over the hill, so she was grateful that she still did have work. She smiled at the thought of the bonuses – free rolls and buns from the morning job, a fish tea every Friday and Saturday night, and a tinkle on the piano when she dusted the keyboard.

There was no need for Patsy to knock at Dinah's door since the key was in the lock. That was no great surprise as Dinah found it easier for people to let themselves in rather than her having the bother of going to open the door. However, when Patsy advanced into the living room (which in her opinion was in need of a good tidy-up) she was confronted by Etta staggering towards the bathroom with a kettle of boiling water. On seeing Patsy, Etta did a quick about-turn into the kitchen with the dribbling kettle. Patsy's eyes were now drawn to Etta's infant son, Bill, who was rocking on his bottom from side to side on the floor. From the odour emanating from that direction he was obviously in need of a nappy change.

"Is your Bill no needing his hippen changed?" she called through to Etta.

"Aye, I'm just going to do it. Wish he was potty-trained."

"Well, you'll have to work at that – no spend most of the day smoking fags and with your nose in a paper. Look, if you don't change him right now he'll have spread it all not just up his back but right up into his head."

Before Etta could speak, a voice from the bathroom shouted, "Etta, where on earth are you with the hot water? This bath is getting to be bearable . . . and I'm needing the gin topped up."

Etta had re-emerged from the kitchen and Patsy was surprised when she skipped over the floor, lifted up Bill and then fled out of the front door.

"Etta, you dozy besom," cried Dinah, "you're supposed to be helping me with my problem. But right now you're only hindering me. Now get in here pronto with that water."

When the bathroom door was kicked fully open, Dinah drew her feet up from the bottom of the bath so they wouldn't be scalded when the boiling water was poured in.

But it wasn't the water that sent Dinah's temperature soaring. It was the sight of her mother who, despite the limited daylight coming though the semi-blacked-out window, immediately knew what was going on. Without uttering a word, Patsy plunged a hand into the scalding water, fished out the plug and sent the water cascading away. "What *do* you think you're doing?" screamed Dinah while trying to grab the stopper from her mother.

"Trying to save your soul from eternal damnation," shouted her mother vehemently, as she grabbed a towel and began to rub Dinah's back dry. "And why I'm bothering I don't know, because writhing in purgatory or burning in hell forever more is a sight too good for you!"

Dinah's head slumped forward and she began to sob uncontrollably. "Mum. Don't you realise I'll be a laughing-stock?" she cried.

"Well, wouldn't that be preferable to eternal damnation?" retorted Patsy.

"You don't understand." Dinah hesitated as she searched for an excuse that would have her mother relent. "I was taken advantage of by a . . ." She just couldn't continue.

"A GI Joe?" sneered Patsy, seizing the gin bottle and pouring the remaining contents into the lavatory, flushing it away with a defiant pull of the chain.

Dinah nodded. "So you see, it would be better to risk damnation and get rid of it."

"What?" screeched Patsy. "Look, Dinah, if you, a married woman, hadn't been keeping company with that blasted man, he couldn't have . . . well he just *couldn't* have!"

"But Mum, you seem to think I don't know I've sinned and now am going to commit an even bigger sin – a mortal one – that three Hail Marys and an hour on my knees

praying won't get me out of. But I *have* to do something."
Dinah could see from the look on her mother's face that
Patsy was going to take a lot more convincing before she'd
let her abort the baby so she continued quickly, "Don't you
see that I'd rather be doomed for ever than what it would do
to . . . Oh, Mum, think how Tam would feel when he gets
home – and he *will* get home now that we're winning."
Dinah looked imploringly at her mother but still there was
no sign of weakening from Patsy so she hurriedly added,
"Not to mention the disgrace on the bairns."

"I *am* thinking about Tam and the bairns and all the
heartache you'll cause them. But more important, I'm
thinking of *myself* because if I did let you do such a mortal
sin I would be condemned too!" Dinah looked as if she was
about to interrupt her mother but changed her mind and
Patsy continued her tirade: "So the best solution is for you
to go to the Sisters in Glasgow where nobody will know
who you are – and what you are. The bairn, God bless him
or her, can be adopted from there."

Dinah leapt out of the bath. "You sanctimonious old
witch. You would send me, your only daughter, to a St
Jude's Laundry where the vicious nuns will beat the living
daylights oot of me until they think I'm no longer in moral
danger!"

"Who says the Holy Sisters are cruel?"

"Who says? Just have a look at Sadie Thomson, raped by
her father and he's still abusing his daughters at will. She
was sent to Glasgow to give birth to her bairn and she'll
never be the same again." Dinah shook her head. "Mammy,
they say Sadie's so crazed noo, always looking for the bairn
that's God knows where, that they're thinking she'll need to
go to Bangour Village Hospital!"

"Dinah, the choice is yours."

"But it's no. I want to abort this," Dinah looked down at her stomach, "and you're only thinking of yourself and your conscience by making me have it."

"Yes. And, as I've said, the choice is either you thole all the embarrassment – and can I remind you that I'll have to put up with that too – or you go to the nuns!"

8

Even now, in October 1943, Fred Armstrong couldn't really say the men had settled into the fertile farmland surroundings of Frankvitz, which they'd reached after their gruelling march of some 550 kilometres through Poland in June 1941. They just hadn't been able to understand why they had been moved. They'd worked very hard in the sugar-beet factory and although their diet was poor and the conditions appalling they had caused no trouble. They were even grateful that the stability meant they occasionally got letters from home and had been given access three times to their looted Red Cross parcels!

The surprising thing about the farmland was that it was also being worked by Polish male along with Russian male and *female* prisoners of war. At the end of the day the four different groups would trudge wearily towards their designated huts for the night.

Normally the chat there would always come around to exchanging ideas on how to escape, though to be realistic there was no way that anyone could escape and survive. So it caused much amusement when Billy announced that he thought they should try to dig a tunnel. His mates thought Billy hadn't quite grasped that you didn't have to dig a tunnel to get out of farmland – you just had to walk out when the guards weren't looking. Fred had gone out of his way to tell all that to Billy, who in turn shook his head and patiently went on to explain that he wouldn't be digging a tunnel in order to escape – but to get into the Russian women's sleeping quarters at night!

Christmas 1943 was just three days away when Fred found himself putting his bony fingers to his face and savagely massaging his sunken cheeks. He was desperate to avert his mind from the problem in front of him. Oh yes, he did try to work miracles for his men, but Charlie, brave and always optimistic Charlie Tracey, just wasn't going to make it. The trouble for Charlie, and indeed for all of them, was that, having been force-marched from their first camp to this farmland, the long trek, the starvation diet and all the other deprivations had taken their harsh toll. And that was on top of the years spent in captivity. No one, no matter how tall, now weighed more than six-and-a-half stone. This meant they were susceptible to all types of infection and in particular to the dysentery that was rife within the camp.

Fred had nursed Charlie through his first bout of dysentery, but this second one would, he feared, take him away.

"Sarge," asked Charlie, whose voice was so weak that Fred had to lean over to hear, "any letters . . . from hame? I just ken my ma would have written at least once since my birthday last April."

Lifting himself from Charlie's bed, Fred gave a nod of assent before striding out of the bunk house and calling to one of the guards. "Look," he said to the big abusive Bulgarian who had taken the job of guarding the prisoners rather than be shot, "that young lad in there, Charlie Tracey, is dying and he was asking if there were any letters for him. Could you check?"

"You maybe pay me something for my trouble?" replied the guard in broken English.

"No! But won't all the stuff you and your mates have taken from our Red Cross parcels no be enough, like? The parcels and their contents are all we have to trade with right now." Fred now looked straight into the guard's eyes. He hoped the man could read in his steely stare that he was telling him they wouldn't always be prisoners and that they both knew how the war was going to end.

Half an hour had gone by before the guard returned, clutching a bundle of letters. "Here," he said with a big smirk on his face. "Look how good I am to you! I have even brought two Red Cross parcels for you to divide among you all."

Fred smiled his thanks and began to skim through the letters. All had been posted about two months previously and he wondered what had happened to the ones that would have gone to their first Stalag. He shook his head, thinking it was better to have a few letters than none at all. Luckily, there were two for Charlie and Fred held them up for him to see. "Aye," said the dying man, "that's Ma's handwriting. Beautiful, is it no?" He then started to cough and retch before falling backwards and closing his eyes. Fred didn't realise for a few minutes that he had gone, but then he tore open the envelopes and, taking out the letters, read them to Charlie. If only, he thought, the old myth was true that the spirit didn't leave the body for half an hour after death and that Charlie was hearing his mother's words.

The men were disheartened by the loss of Charlie but death in the camp was an all too common occurrence and they accepted it stoically. The divvying up of the Red Cross parcels helped to blunt their grief, especially as those who smoked could now share a cigarette – their first smoke for a year. Those who had letters from home read out juicy items of news. However, pleased as he was to get as many as six letters, Tam was rather put out that no one had said a word about how his darling Phyllis was faring. He felt shocked by the family's callousness and scanned the letters again – but no – not even Dinah (whose two letters began, "Dear Tam," and then were heavily censored since, no doubt, she'd written about how the war was going and ended: "Missing you so much, darling. Your ever-loving wife, Dinah.") mentioned Phyllis.

His mother's letter was all about how hard Dod was finding the conditions in Saughton Prison where you had to buy your own fags and how she was sure Tam would be outraged at such cruelty. Then there was a letter from his son Johnny who, like his mother, had almost all of his letter censored so that Tam couldn't tell whether he'd mentioned Phyllis. Finally there was a letter from Senga, who could now write beautifully but was only eager that he should know how many eggs the hens had laid – and he didn't know, because the number, which the Germans must have thought was propaganda that would have given heart to the prisoners, had been blacked out!

Tam was still pondering about Phyllis when Billy Morrison grabbed his own letters and then rubbed the one from his dearest chaste sweetheart, Violet, against his chest before beginning to read it. Everyone was startled when Billy, instead of offering his usual refrain of, "Oh lads, listen. She loves me! She does! Keeping herself pure for me, so she is. Dreams, she does, of our wedding night!" suddenly leapt from his bed and screamed, "Jessie Bell! Jessie Bell!"

"Who in the name of heavens is Jessie Bell?" asked Tam, grabbing hold of Billy and trying to calm him.

"No other," sobbed Billy, throwing the letter to the floor, "than my Violet!"

Fred bent down, picked up the letter and began to read it. "The bitch – she sure is a bloody Jezebel!"

"What's wrong?" the others chorused.

"Gone off with another man?" asked Tam.

"Aye. But the man in question went right off her . . . when she told him she was in the pudding club!" said Fred.

"And there's no way his wife back in Toronto will let him change his mind!" added Andy who had taken the letter from Fred.

George McIntyre started to laugh before spluttering, "Oh Billy, do tell us. Do! Did she willingly invite him in to deflower her or did he have to dig a tunnel first?"

9

The school room was, as usual, being decorated for the festive season. While Senga was helping Mrs Carruthers put the finishing touches to the tree, she suddenly asked, "Do you think this will be our last Christmas here, Miss?"

"Well things are going a lot better for us in the war, but I think it might be a while yet before it's all over."

"You know, Miss, I still cannae believe I'm here in this braw hoose. I mean, it's like a fairytale, living in this castle, so it is." Mrs Carruthers smiled because she, like the children, was sometimes overawed by the grandeur of the Craigs and its surroundings. "See, when I get back to Hermitage Park School and tell them about this place, nobody's going to believe me. They'll think it's another of my dreams."

"Dreams, Senga? What do you dream about?"

"Well, Miss, I'd love to be like my sister Tess, and get a good job. She's working in the Store Chemist in Newhaven now. Comes home smelling of nice things. And if a bath cube gets broken in the shop she gets to take it hame." Senga became wistful. "And when Johnny leaves here in April he's going to be an apprentice joiner in Henry Robb's."

"Henry Robb's?"

"Aye, ye ken, the shipbuilding place in Leith."

"That's fine for your brother and sister but we know that you're a clever girl and you could be doing much better for yourself than serving in a shop."

Senga sighed. "You maybe think I'm clever, Miss, but

when I get back to Hermitage Park that Miss Irvine will haul me into her duffers' class. I know she will."

A loud hammering at the front door prevented Mrs Carruthers from answering directly, but turning away from Senga she called out over her shoulder, "You're no duffer, Senga, so stop thinking like that or you really will end up becoming one. Now I must go. That will be the new boy I was telling you about."

Senga remembered Mrs Carruthers telling them that some European refugee children who were *bilingual* (which Senga thought was the name of the country they came from) were being sent to the Craigs and that everybody must be nice to them and help them settle in.

A few minutes later Mrs Carruthers returned with a woman dressed in a Red Cross uniform and a young boy about Elsie's age.

"Hello," said Senga enthusiastically, having taken an immediate liking to him.

The boy smiled and replied, "I'm Robert and I'm a Jew."

"Are you?" Senga was quick to respond. "I'm Senga and I'm a Glass!"

10

Patsy had spent some time making herself look respectable. Dark coat, new lisle thread stockings, and shoes that not only were sensible but *looked* sensible; hair tied back and no make-up – not even her precious lipstick. All this was to impress the nuns, whom Father O'Riley had contacted on her behalf. Those nuns, judged to be saints by Patsy, were the ones who would be looking after Dinah while she gave birth – probably within the next two weeks. They'd also arrange for the baby to be immediately baptised and then adopted. They did know, however, that after the birth Patsy would take Dinah home, and accept full responsibility thereafter for Dinah's moral behaviour!

With bowed head, Patsy made her way down Restalrig Road towards Dinah's home in Restalrig Circus, congratulating herself on having saved her daughter's soul. The baby would obviously go to a couple who wanted a child. God, she knew, worked in mysterious ways and, because it was all His will, everything would end up just fine.

At the start of the pregnancy, it had been quite an ordeal keeping Dinah's condition secret, especially when people asked whether Dinah had developed a cyst. Patsy would then insist (in all honesty) that it was just a wee cyst-like problem that would be sorted out quite soon. The hardest part had been during the last ten weeks when Dinah, because of her bulging belly that couldn't be mistaken for anything other than a pregnancy, had never left the house.

But today, April the first, Dinah and Patsy would slink away from the house under cover of darkness and then make their way to Glasgow.

Patsy had just reached Hay's grocery store when she was wrong-footed by encountering Mary, Dinah's hoodwinked mother-in-law, emerging from the shop.

"Oh, it's yourself, Patsy. Sure, here's you all dressed up like you must be going to a funeral." Patsy, thinking life would be so much easier if she *were* going to a funeral, just smiled.

"And how's Dinah? You'd think they doctors would know by now exactly what's up with her."

"Oh," replied Patsy with a smile. "She's going into hospital to . . ." she nearly said "today" but that would have caused Mary to wonder since hospitals only admitted emergencies at night, so she hurriedly added, ". . . tomorrow."

"Good! Now, Patsy, did I tell you that Dod actually tried to get himself bunged up again?" Patsy nodded. "But, poor soul, even though he was caught raiding the NAAFI they've still sent him back to the front line. Thank goodness my Tam's getting it easier, being a prisoner of war. I told you I had a letter from him?" Patsy nodded. "Great that he's able to write now – even uses big words I dinnae quite understand masel."

It took Patsy another five minutes before she could tear herself away from Mary. Dear, gullible Mary, who just loved to go on about all her worries. Dear Mary, whom Patsy knew that if she ever found out about Dinah's little . . . indiscretion . . . would be upset at first but eventually accept it without rancour.

On entering Dinah's living room, Patsy was pleased to

see a suitcase waiting to be picked up. However, there was no sign of Dinah, only Etta.

"Where's Dinah?" asked Patsy, craning her neck to see if her daughter was in the kitchen.

"She's in the bathroom. Been upset all day she has."

"That right?"

"Aye, the very thought of they nuns, even for just two weeks, is enough to give anyone the collie-wobbles."

Patsy huffed with annoyance before going into the bathroom. Dinah was resting against the bath and breathing deeply.

"Now, my lady, if you think you can put on a show and that somehow I won't make you go to Glasgow – you have another thought coming."

As another pain gripped her, Dinah gasped and Patsy gulped, "Here, don't tell me you're in blinking labour?"

Dinah nodded silently before reminding her mother that her labours were always quite short. So short in fact that they were unlikely to get to Edinburgh's Waverley Station tonight, never mind Glasgow's Queen Street, before she gave birth.

"Etta," Patsy cried, "come and give me a hand. Now, Dinah, you just keep breathing deeply and Etta and I will see to you."

As soon as Etta became aware of the problem, she pointed out that they had nothing ready since they hadn't expected the birth to be in the house.

"Doesn't matter," snapped Patsy, grabbing Dinah round the waist and dragging her towards the bedroom. "Just get the kettle and pots filled up and then put them all on the gas. Any clean towels?"

Etta nodded towards the airing cupboard above the water

tank. Once Patsy had Dinah undressed and in bed, she went back to the cupboard but instead of clean towels all she found were six pairs of nylons and three bars of chocolate. She sighed, asking herself if that was all her daughter's favours had cost – six pairs of nylons and some chocolate. Then she became aware that Etta had hurriedly left the house and was now returning with a bundle of towels, nappies and baby clothes which she signalled were all for Dinah. Between contractions, Dinah, to Patsy's consternation, kept asking Etta if she'd collected all the maternity gear because she was expecting (or perhaps hoping for) another German raid.

Two hours later a healthy ten-pound baby boy was born. Of course, he should have been taken immediately for adoption but the moment Patsy looked at him she knew no one would want to be seen pushing a pram with him in it. But reluctantly she had to admit that, of all Dinah's six children, he was by far the most beautiful. Oh yes! GI Joe was a perfect specimen of babyhood.

By now Dinah was sitting up and gesturing to her mother that she wanted to hold her baby. Patsy dutifully handed him over.

"Oh, Mum," sobbed Dinah, "we just can't let him end up in some home where he might be abused and ridiculed."

Patsy nodded in agreement. "Yeah. A right April fool he's made of us all. But as no one will adopt him and you're right – he's our own flesh and blood – so, black as he is, we'll keep him. Wish you'd told us that his dad was a darkie."

Dinah wondered if Patsy now regretted that she'd stopped her from aborting Joe but, while she cuddled her son close into herself, she smiled because she hadn't. She was so utterly besotted with this angelic child that she was willing to take all the punishment that she knew would be coming her way.

11

To everyone's surprise, Elsie and Robert Wise had struck up a special friendship from their very first meeting. This came about when a tearful Robert confided to her that his father and mother were lost somewhere in Germany and that the Nazis were not very good to the Jews.

"Snap!" Elsie replied. "My Daddy is lost in Germany too and my Granny Glass says that she hopes he's being treated right but she doubts it."

Eleven months on, the pair were now kindred spirits and Elsie was dreading having to ruin things. "Robert," she said tentatively, while she watched him trying to trace a fox's footprints in the hoar frost on the grass just beyond the gravel path at the outside door. "Come back a minute," she continued. "I've got a secret to tell you."

Robert, a puzzled frown on his face, stopped and slowly walked back towards her. "A *real* secret?" he asked.

Elsie nodded. "And it's nice for me but not nice for us."

Robert's quizzical frown gave way to a concerned scowl. "Are you going to say you don't want to be a friend of mine any more because I'm a . . . ?"

"*No!* . . . I'll always be your pal," Elsie exclaimed before blurting out, "It's just that now the war is nearly over and we won't be bombed again, my Mammy says she's going to take us home before Christmas."

The two children now sat down on the outdoor step, each deep in thought. Both were resting their elbows on their knees, faces cupped in their hands. They didn't even look up when the bell sounded to end the morning break and it wasn't until they had to stand up to let the other children pass that they stopped daydreaming.

"You two lost a shilling and found a farthing?" asked Senga, before disappearing into the house.

"No, Senga," wailed Elsie. "It's just that Robert will be so lonely when I go home."

"Sssh," Senga ordered. "You know that's top-secret because Granny Kelly mightn't let Mammy take us back."

"Right enough," chortled Elsie, "that's what we could do."

"Do what?"

"Get Granny Kelly to ask Mammy to take Robert in and be her son just like she did with Joe." Elsie now turned to Robert. "Our Joe is a wee chocolate-coloured baby that nobody wanted, so Granny asked Mammy to take him in and now he's one of us!"

"Oh, that would be just great," said Robert, as he stood up and jumped for joy. "But it would only be till my father and mother come back and take me home."

"You've got no other folks?" asked Senga, who was not entirely convinced that the story of Joe having been left on Granny Kelly's doorstep was true.

"Well, I do have a grandmother who's somewhere in London."

"Poor London was always getting battered. You were better here with us, Robert."

Robert nodded but hesitated before saying, "To be truthful, the Red Cross lady said she would take me to my grandmother when the war is over."

* * *

The birth of baby Joe, although an acute embarrassment for Dinah when he was first taken out in his pram, had brought out a fierce protective instinct that she had never shown with any of her other children – not even Phyllis. There was no doubt she loved all of her children but their needs had seemed to come second to her own unfailing desire to socialise. When it came to Joe, however, she made all the supreme sacrifices – never once going out at night to a dance hall or pub – so when the telegram arrived at her mother-in-law's house, saying that her son Dod had been killed in action, Dinah had raced over to Mary's house to comfort her.

"Mary," she said, as she entered the house and found her sitting at the table staring into space. "I'm so sorry, darling. What a price you've paid for this bloody war."

Mary sat shaking her head. "He was a rogue," she mumbled. "I know that – but he was *my* rogue – my lovable wee devil." Tears were now cascading down Mary's cheeks and all she could do was sniffle through them. "Always wondered where I went wrong with him. I mean, how could I have steered him better? Losing him, my lovely wee boy, is the price I have to pay for being a bad mother."

Dinah looked around, hoping to see her father-in-law Jack, but he was nowhere to be seen. No doubt, she thought, he'll be consoling himself in the nearest hostelry instead of being here, comforting his distraught wife.

"Look, Mary," she coaxed, "why don't you come over to my house and let me look after you?"

Mary spat through her tears, "You think, you actually *think*, I'll feel better looking at your wee black bastard who'll break my Tam's heart when he comes home?" She roughly shoved Dinah's hand away before pushing her chair back, standing up and with a shaking finger signalled to Dinah to get out of the house.

Two days later Dinah was surprised when her mother, red-faced and breathless, rushed into her house, grabbed Joe, swung him around her waist and headed for the outside door. "Quick, Dinah, you've got to come over to Mary's place and give me a hand." Patsy hesitated before adding, as her eyes looked upwards: "Oh, Holy Mary Mother of God, help us in our hour of need!"

"Me go over to that old witch's house after what she called my bairn? Said he was a wee black bastard!" screeched Dinah as she struggled to wrestle Joe from her mother.

Before answering, Patsy firmly kicked the door shut. "Look," she hoarsely whispered through gritted teeth, "Mary's been a damn fine mother-in-law to you and the poor soul's at the end of her tether." Patsy looked surreptitiously about before lowering her voice and muttering, "Look, walls in these bleeding stairs have ears so you just take my word for it that Mary's in deep trouble. She needs help and you're coming with me to give her it!"

"And do you think, now that we know that her accepting my wee Joe was all a kid-on . . ."

"She put a brave face on it because she wanted to support me and now she's needing our help. So we're going."

Without another word, Patsy opened the door once again and, despite her age and excess weight, raced all the way over from Restalrig Circus to Mary's house in Restalrig Road and then took the stairs to Mary's second-floor flat two at a time.

Entering the house, Patsy was pleased to see Tess wiping

her grandmother's face with a wet cloth and gently patting her cheeks, while pleading, "Oh, Granny Mary, please don't go to sleep again. Please don't – because Granny Patsy says if I let you fall asleep you'll die. Oh, Granny Mary, I don't want you to die!"

By now Dinah had joined her mother and daughter in the room where all the windows, even in the December chill and ruthless wind, had been flung open wide. Yet there was still a cloying smell hanging about.

"What's happened?" asked Dinah, as the choking gas fumes assailed her nostrils and almost choked her.

Patsy had now taken over from Tess to whom she handed Joe. "Couldn't take any more. No, she just couldn't. So she tried to . . ." Patsy hesitated, unable to say the word "kill" and eventually whispered, "So she tried to harm herself."

"Lucky she only had tuppence for the meter," sniffed Tess. "And wi' gas that dear just now, you need at least fourpence to end it all."

Dinah was about to say she could have lent her a couple of pennies but the look on her mother's face deterred her.

"Right," said Patsy, who was now in control. "Tess, you've been a great help and thank goodness you came in to see your Granny on your way home and then you ran for me, but now you'll help us best if you take Joe home and look after him. Don't want him being made sick with they fumes. And don't worry. Your Mammy and I will look after Granny Mary."

"We will. Oh, I see what you mean – you want me to go over to the phone box at Glen's Post Office and phone for a doctor or an ambulance."

There was no mistaking the look of horror on Patsy's face but before answering Dinah she said firmly, "Off you go, Tess, and remember to tell nobody about what has gone on in here today. Stay loyal to your Granny Mary and keep your mouth shut."

Once Tess had left with Joe, Patsy immediately began to haul Mary to her feet and as soon as she had her standing upright, wheeled her head around to face Dinah – and Dinah was left in no doubt, by the utter contempt on her mother's face, that she was in for a right ear-bashing. "Dinah," Patsy spat, while stroking Mary's drooping head, "don't you realise that if you get a doctor or anyone, poor Mary here will end up in prison? Is that what you really want? You callous bitch!"

Dinah laughed derisively. "Prison?"

"Yes! Surely you know it's a criminal offence to try and commit suicide. You end up in jail – no to mention coming out with a criminal record."

"And what do they do to them that manage to end it all?"

"You know fine what happens to them, Dinah. They can't be buried on hallowed ground! And their soul is condemned to purgatory for ever!"

Mary started to sway while her head and eyes rolled. "Just let me sleep. Please just let me, let me . . . sle-ee-p," she mumbled as her legs began to buckle beneath her.

"Look," argued Dinah forcefully, "if her life's so blooming awful – and she's not Catholic, so committing suicide isn't a mortal sin and her soul won't be forever in purgatory – then why don't you just let her . . ."

Patsy nearly let Mary go as she lashed out at Dinah. "You unfeeling pig," she shrieked. "Mary here is a poor soul whose patience has been tried beyond endurance and she's my friend." She inhaled deeply before adding contemptuously, "Forbye she's your guid-mother. And don't you forget, my girl, that your wanton behaviour's partly responsible for pushing her over the edge the day." Patsy paused and crossed herself before going on. "And because of that I feel responsible for never having properly got to grips with you!"

Knowing that she would be unable to score any points over her mother, Dinah simply stood like a statue and sighed while her mother went on vehemently. "So I'll have no more back-chat from you. And come over here, right now, and help me get Mary down the stairs and round to Hawkhill playing fields."

They'd only just opened the door and were about to step out into the common stair when they heard footsteps.

"Quick," urged Patsy, slamming the door shut again. "We'll wait till the coast's clear."

"Why?" asked Dinah.

"Because it's enough to know your own sorrows without broadcasting them," Patsy replied. "Besides, I know how Mary feels about losing her son." Patsy's thoughts then drifted back to the heartbreak she'd suffered when all the children she'd carried for nine months had, with the exception of Dinah, never breathed a breath.

Both women stayed silent until no more sounds could be heard from outside. When they judged it to be safe, Patsy reached out to open the door but stopped abruptly when Dinah asked, "Why are we going round to Hawkhill playing fields? Surely it would be better to keep her here where no one will see her."

Patsy sighed again. "What? Can you no smell the gas in here? The windows have been opened ever since I came in and the place is still stinking and claustrophobic." Dinah cast her eyes upwards once again as her mother continued, "No one will be there at this time of day playing football or hockey – so that means we'll be able to walk her round the pitches in the fresh air until she's fully recovered!"

"And how long will that take?" demanded Dinah, as she opened the door.

"As long as it takes," hissed her mother, pushing Mary forward. "Probably . . . two or three hours . . . at least!"

12

The relentless wind tore at the clothes that five years in captivity had rendered ragged and useless to protect the emaciated forms of those who had survived the hospitality of the German prisoner of war camps – the infamous Stalags where the norm for prisoners was either to be worked to death or killed by starvation. And if that wasn't bad enough, the resilient men of the British Army, who had been taken prisoners in June 1940, just after Dunkirk, had now been trudging for a whole month – from 16 February to 19 March 1945 – either in bare feet just swaddled in cloth or in well-worn clogs they had manufactured for themselves, their army boots having long ago disintegrated with the long forced march into captivity.

This new trek had been a consequence of the German guards realising that if they did not move the prisoners (whom they hoped to use as a bargaining tool) towards the advancing American army they would have to surrender to the Russians, who were relentlessly advancing from the east.

Fred could fully understand why the Germans didn't wish to hand themselves over to the Russians, whose mother-country they'd invaded and who were guilty of the most inhumane treatment, not only of Soviet soldiers but also of civilians.

What he couldn't understand was why they should have embarked on a march they knew would take over a month when they were aware they couldn't even supply their prisoners with enough drinking water, never mind food or shelter. There was also the continual air bombardment from the Allied forces, which had the men diving for any cover they could find.

Irate shouts of, "Well, that's it then," emanating from Tam Glass and Eddie Gibson put an end to Fred's marching forward and he wheeled about to face his men.

"What's the problem?" he asked. "Surely Billy Morrison hasn't gone AWOL again." Fred was referring to Billy's bold escapades to find any food or indeed anything that could be used to make life easier. Escapades that were growing ever bolder as the German guards became lax, due to their realisation that it would soon be themselves who would be marching along with rifles at their backs.

"Naw," replied Tam. "Look!"

Fred's eyes were focused on the small horse that had willingly carried the cooking pots and bedding. She was now lying prostrate on the ground, quite obviously dead. "Poor sod," he thought. "Like ourselves, over-worked and starved beyond endurance!"

"What'll we do now?" asked Eddie as he began to unload pots and blankets from the animal.

"Well, as we've not had a decent meal for months, how about we find Billy who was an apprentice butcher before the war and get him to carve up the beast and then we'll have a real good feed tonight!" suggested Fred. To his surprise there was not a single word of dissent. Funny, he thought, how five years of deprivation can sort out your qualms!

Two days later they arrived at Rawtow POW camp, just a few miles from the front line where American troops were pushing back the remnants of the German army, most of whom were now little more than schoolboys.

Fred and his men were surprised the next morning when they awoke to find that their guards had deserted them, having decided to make a run for the American line and surrender. Taking time to consider what it would be best to do, Fred suggested to his men that it would be safest to stay where they were. "Here," he said, looking about the camp, "we've got shelter and since we haven't any arms we can't take on the German army. Food," he continued, looking at the emaciated men before him, "is going to be scarce but maybe the good feed we had from the horse will keep us going . . ." Most of the men shook their heads in disbelief and rubbed their hands over their swollen bellies, while Fred continued, "Okay, a feed which also gave most of us a good dose of the skitters!" He now looked directly at Billy. "But a feed we've had nevertheless and so – along with whatever can be foraged outside the camp by our expert here – we'll keep going. We're nearly there, lads," he pleaded. "Just a few more days – maybe only hours!" Billy bowed his head in acknowledgement. "That's settled then – we've decided to survive *here* until the Americans arrive!"

There was no spoken response from the men. They'd survived thus far by following Fred's orders to the letter and they would continue to do so until they finally arrived home in Scotland.

The men all took refuge in their own thoughts. Eddie thought of Betty and his dad. What would be their reaction to his return? Had their feelings towards him changed in the space of five years? Had Betty found someone else? It had been months since there had been any letters from home.

Stretching out his hands in front of himself, he gazed sadly at them, feeling they were the hands of a much older man. With their hacks, ingrained dirt and broken nails, they were almost skeletal and it would take years perhaps for them to recover. His eyes then turned to look down at his shoeless feet. Black and twisted nails stared back at him. He smiled to himself, wondering who would believe that he and young Billy were the only ones left with their black toenails – all the others had lost theirs in the last two weeks.

Tam Glass's thoughts were now miles away in Restalrig Circus. Dinah, his own Dinah, was first in his thoughts. He inhaled deeply, as if taking in the scent of her perfume. Right at that moment he just couldn't remember if it had been Mischief or Evening in Paris that she favoured – it didn't matter though: he was so intoxicated by the thought of being with her again that the heady bouquet of the scent invaded his nostrils. His dreamlike trance had him remember how she looked when they'd danced together. He shifted his back and squirmed with pleasure, wondering what it might feel like to have her massage all the weariness from his body. He smiled as he reckoned that five years of weariness and abuse would certainly take more than one treatment to ease. His thoughts then went to his children. They would all be five years older now. Would the youngest of them remember anything at all about him? "No matter," he reasoned to himself. "I'll soon make up for lost time and spend every minute I can with them. And with Phyllis, my poor paralysed Phyllis, who's suffered far more than I ever have!" Tears welled up in his eyes and he brushed the drips from his nose with the back of his hand before going on with his daydreams. "Never mind, I can just see myself pushing her bed-chair out into the fresh air and up to

Lochend Park." He chuckled and licked his dry, cracked lips. "We'll have so much extra bread we'll be able to throw a few crumbs to the ducks in the pond."

Billy too was dreaming. His thoughts were of what his homecoming would have been like if Violet, his childhood sweetheart, had only stayed faithful and waited for him. He sighed as he admitted to himself, "She's no longer a virgin though. Didn't keep herself pure for me as she promised." He looked disdainfully at his blackened toes and spindly, scabby legs. "I'm hardly what she'd call a catch now. And I suppose that now she's a mother there'll be no place in her life for a wreck like me."

Fred too was thinking but his thoughts weren't of home. He'd joined the army because there hadn't been much of a home life for him except with his younger sister Eileen. He gazed upon the silent thoughtful group who'd been his family for these last five years. Their welfare, he admitted, had been all-important to him – trying to do his best for them; keeping them alive; keeping their spirits up – that was what had kept Fred going when it would have been easier to throw in the towel. What now? Would he ever be able to live an ordinary life without these men? Tears came to Fred's eyes. This was the soft side of Fred, the tough soldier who could make the most distasteful of decisions and get on with it, always provided it was in the best interests of *his* men!

At 10pm precisely, on 2 May 1945, the first of the liberating American army entered the Stalag. Fred and his men ran from their huts to greet them. Then they fell to their knees, raised their hands towards heaven and shouted, "Freedom! Freedom! Freedom! At last we're free."

The Americans, who (it was wildly rumoured) were always amply supplied with food, chocolate and nylons – though what use nylons would be on the front line was anybody's guess – were delighted not only to liberate the men but also to put an end to their many privations.

On 10 May 1945, two days before the official end of the Second World War, the men had their last view of Germany, when the aeroplane carrying them home circled high above the flattened cities beside the river Rhine. As they looked down upon the devastation, no one shed a single tear for any German soldier, woman or child who had suffered from the ruin inflicted on them by the Allies.

By 11 May 1945 the men were safely installed at Worthing Camp where showers, toothpaste and brushes, clothes and medical treatments were freely available to them for the first time in five years.

As was to be expected, Billy quickly suggested to one of the nurses that he was quite unable to wash himself without physical assistance. "No problem," was her reply as she promptly called on a six-foot, fourteen-stone male orderly to carry out the task!

13

There was not a single person living in Restalrig Circus or the surrounding area who had not made some contribution to the street party on VE Day to celebrate the ending of the war.

The children could hardly contain their excitement as they watched the long trestle tables, borrowed from the YMCA, being set up in the square just outside the gates to the allotments. The tables were then decorated with crêpe paper and every family had donated sandwiches, baked scones or fairy cakes – while it was rumoured that lemonade and red cola would flow like rivers. Even Ice Cream Johnny, who had been let out of custody since he was no longer considered a threat to national security, was going to put in an appearance on his ice cream cart. And every child was to be given a penny ice cream cone smothered in raspberry sauce!

So far as they could (because new clothes still required clothing coupons), the mothers had dressed the children up. Some looked quite comical in dresses and trousers that were either too big or too small for them. But most of the girls had brightly coloured crêpe paper bows adorning their hair and all the boys sported school ties.

The excitement was reaching fever pitch as the children took their places on the wooden benches and began to stuff as much food as they could into their mouths.

"Great to see them all enjoying themselves. At last we can be sure they won't be blasted to smithereens in any air raid," Patsy remarked to Dinah.

Dinah, who was holding young Joe tightly in her arms, simply nodded.

"You no pleased the blinking war is over?"

Dinah silently nodded again. "Oh, Mammy, just think. Next week at this time Tam could be home."

"Aye, and is that no what we all want – especially you and his mother Mary?"

"But Mammy, what about wee Joe here? I mean, how do I explain him away? There's no way he won't eventually find out that I'm his mammy."

Patsy looked at her daughter, thinking shouldn't she have thought about that when she'd started cavorting with a . . . She was about to say "black GI" but, as was usual with her, she softened it to "coloured soldier" – or had it been an airman? Didn't matter anyway. The man was long gone and had no intention of coming back. "Look," she said after a long pause, "how about me taking Joe to bide with me? That way he won't be a constant reminder to Tam of your . . ." Here she paused, trying to find a more descriptive word than infidelity.

Sensing her mother's dilemma, Dinah spat out, "Whoring?"

"Precisely! But *you* said it. Not me."

"No. Joe is mine and no matter what price I have to pay I'm keeping him by me."

"Think, my lassie, that cost might be beyond even what . . ."

Before she could finish, Senga ran up to them. "Quick, Mammy, give me Joe. He's to be at the party too." With that, Senga grabbed Joe from her mother and carried him over to the table she'd just left.

"Funny how quickly Senga has taken to Joe. Proper little mother she is to him," observed Dinah.

"Aye," mused her mother. "You never see her now except he's with her. I think he's filled the gap that Phyllis's passing left!"

14

An uneasy silence had fallen on the occupants in all the carriages of the special train they'd boarded at Kings Cross Station in London. Every seat was taken by those very special travellers – ordinary men, who had done the extraordinary and stayed behind in France so that their comrades waiting on the beaches of Dunkirk could be rescued and taken safely back to Britain. Those who had reached safety in this way were able to take up the fight again in 1944 and, aided by the Americans, eventually gained the hard-fought victory – the triumph that thankfully had secured the release of those men now on the train.

All the passengers seemed afraid to look at one other. They rubbed their hands together, whistled quietly, stamped their feet and did anything to ease the apprehension they felt as they waited for the guard to blow his whistle and signal that the train was free to depart. Only then could they definitely feel they were on their way home!

As the train trundled its sluggish way through England, the periods of silence gave way to playful banter (much of it unprintable) when the conversation would centre around what they would all be doing this time tomorrow! All took part except Eddie, who was full of doubts. He couldn't bear to think about tomorrow until he had got through today. He sat, staring dumbly out of the window, noting the names of the English towns and cities as they flashed by him. To keep his panic in check he imagined that the wheels of the train were saying, "We're going home. We're going home. We're going home. Betty's waiting. Betty's waiting. Betty's waiting."

Suddenly he saw it – the sign he had longed to see for five years. Turning to his companions, he yelled, "Boys, we're o'er the border. D'ye hear? We're o'er the border, lads. I've just seen the sign that says 'Scotland'!"

"You mean we're back in God's own country?" asked Andy Young, punching the air jubilantly.

Eddie nodded. Silence fell again in the carriage. No one could speak. After a while all that could be heard were the quiet sobs of grown men.

The train had not quite ground to a halt on 13 May 1945, at Edinburgh's Waverley Station, when the carriage doors burst open and the occupants jumped down to the platform to be greeted by their waiting relatives.

Eddie just couldn't believe that not only was Betty there to welcome him but so were her mother and her granny! Billy too was surprised when Violet came running along the platform waving to him and shouting, "I'm here, Billy. Your Mammy's waiting at hame. She hasn't stopped crying since we heard you were on your way back. And look! There's your Dad." Billy didn't embrace Violet but he did run up to his father who was hobbling towards them with the aid of a walking-stick. As they embraced, Billy thought how old his Dad had become. But he knew his Mum and Dad adored him and no doubt not having seen him for five years and wondering how he was faring had taken their toll.

Tam had to push his way through the crowds to get to Dinah, his own Dinah, who appeared to him more beautiful than Lana Turner – but then Lana Turner was only a film star and not his wife! So Dinah should seem lovely to him. After all, she'd spent hours on her appearance – she'd even had White's the hairdresser in the Kirkgate give her a Marcel wave. But, being an expert on cosmetics, she had done the make-up herself and of course her stunning legs were sheathed in a pair of her best sheer nylons that she'd kept specially for this day. "You alone?" Tam asked as he scanned the crowds, hoping to see his mother or some of his children.

"Not quite. No show without Punch!" replied Dinah, pointing with a backward jerk of her thumb.

Tam was now faced with greeting his father, Jack Glass. He knew he should be flattered that his Dad had given up an afternoon at the pub with his drinking cronies but somehow he felt nothing for this man who really was a stranger to him. "How goes it, son?" Jack asked.

"Fine. Just want to get hame to my family and all will be well."

Jack gave a cynical snigger before withering Dinah with a disparaging look. "Ah well, I suppose you best hear it from me . . ."

Tam was about to say, "Hear what?" when he noticed that Fred was leaving the platform alone. It appeared no one had come to meet him but, just as Tam was about to run after him and invite him home, a young attractive woman, whom Tam instinctively knew was Fred's sister Eileen, pushed her way out of the crowd calling, "Fred. Fred! Wait for me."

Jack tried to talk to Tam again and again but Dinah always managed to steer Tam's attention towards herself and finally she whispered to Jack, "I know why you came here today but you won't win. And another thing! I'm paying for a taxi to take us home. You're welcome to ride with us provided you keep your malicious trap shut!"

On reaching Restalrig Circus, Tam was not disappointed. His mother, Mary, and Dinah's mother, Patsy, were both at the gate waving flags, and all his children were out on the pavement. Oh gosh, he thought, how they've grown in five years. Now who's who? The willowy, attractive peroxide blonde just had to be his seventeen-year-old Tess. She was so like Dinah had been at that age – the very age when Tam had been smitten by her. As he cradled Tess in his arms, he felt a tug at his sleeve and looked down at the little girl standing there. She was one of his – but was she Senga or Elsie? "I'm Elsie," the little girl announced, putting an end to his wondering.

"And I'm Johnny," the gangling young man with the broken voice butted in.

Tam released Tess and shook Johnny's hand vigorously before lifting Elsie up and kissing her while he fondled her hair. But what about the others? A diffident young lassie, standing by his mother, smiled to him and he knew instantly that she was Senga. Putting Elsie down, he went over and took both his mother and Senga into his arms. "Good to be home. Good to see you all. I missed you all so much," he mumbled. Then he looked about. There was no bed-chair. Only a trestle table set for a lavish tea. Where was Phyllis hiding? "Where's my Phyllis?" he asked, starting to walk towards the bedroom.

"Oh no!" came the chorus from Dinah, Mary and Patsy.

Tam stopped and turned to face the women. "Oh, Tam, I wrote and told you . . . that she had died."

"Died?" he cried.

"Yes. I wrote and told you. Away back – it was the Christmas of 1941 that the wee soul passed away," Dinah protested. "Did you no get the letter?"

Tam shook his head. He gasped for breath. Mary went over and made him sit down and then, with her arm around his shoulder, she whispered in his ear, "Tam, my son, the bairns have prepared this party for you. Dinnae greet the noo. Try and haud it thegither. The pair o' us will weep thegither the morn." Tam breathed in deeply and raised his head. It was then he saw Etta with a wee boy seated on her knee. "And who's he?"

"Mine," Etta replied with pride.

"Right wee smasher he is too," observed Tam.

Then he saw Joe. "And who do you belong to?" he asked the other small boy who was cheekily beaming in his direction.

"He's mine," Senga answered before anyone could say a word. "A gift from God he is."

Tam leaned back in the chair and looked up at the ceiling. Surely, he argued, his own precious daughter, who was only thirteen, couldn't be the mother of a toddler!

"Look, let's just get on with the welcome-home party," interjected Dinah. "And who belongs to who we can sort out tomorrow."

Patsy nodded her agreement to Mary and both silently acknowledged that tomorrows had a habit of arriving all too soon.

After the welcome home, everyone, except for Tam, either went home or to bed. Tam had urged Dinah to retire, saying he would follow as soon as he could calm all the many emotions he was experiencing.

First, he helped Johnny take down the bed-settee. Then he settled himself in the easy chair and as he watched his sixteen-year-old son quickly fall asleep he realised just what he, and indeed his children, had been cheated of. Feelings that he had had to hold in check during the five years of his captivity were now swamping him. He couldn't stop his thoughts turning to his beloved Phyllis and all he wished was to weep for her. He accepted that the others had gone through their period of grieving and by now they'd grown used to her not being with them – but he had just learned of her death. It felt as if his heart had been pierced with a dagger and that his life-blood was oozing from him. He was now grateful for the dusky twilight because he wanted no one to see the gentle relief brought to him by the tears cascading down his cheeks.

15

Utter exhaustion eventually overcame Tam and he fell asleep for a short time but awoke suddenly at five o'clock to discover the sun streaming in through the kitchen window. After refreshing himself in the bathroom he left home and wandered down Restalrig Road and then across Leith Links, finding himself at length in the dock area that he knew so well. It was only natural that his wanderings took him to Henry Robb's shipyard where he'd first been an apprentice and then a time-served shipwright. He bit his lip and wondered if he could perhaps get a second start there. Already he was planning how best he could support his family once he'd been officially demobbed.

From Henry Robb's, Tam rambled rather aimlessly around the Leith he had known as a child – Couper Street Primary School, David Kilpatrick's Secondary, the Salvation Army Halls, where he had banged the tambourine – all had to be revisited along with the many other places that had known him as a boy. By lunch-time he found himself outside the Black Swan pub, his father's favourite watering-hole, and it was not until three in the afternoon that he finally arrived home.

On opening the door, Tam was immediately greeted by his mother and Dinah, surrounded by all the children.

"Where on earth have you been?" demanded Dinah furiously.

"We've been beside oursels with worry," added his mother.

Tam took a deep breath before giving his orders. "Right now! All you bairns, get outside and play." Dinah and Mary exchanged glances with each other. "And you, Mammy, you get back to your own house. I've things to thrash out with Dinah."

"You've had your feet in the sawdust with your Dad?"

Tam nodded. Dinah couldn't hide her apprehension.

"Look, Tam, this bloody war has made all of us do things we wish we hadnae," pleaded his mother.

"You been whoring with the darkies an aw?"

Mary shook her head. "Naw. But if it hadnae been for Dinah, and even more for Patsy, I wouldnae be here the day. They saved my life, son, so they did." Tam was unmoved, so Mary continued, "I tried to end it all after yer brother was slaughtered. Never thought about you and Archie, I didnae. And okay, we ken ye're mad about wee Joe – but he's a braw wee laddie."

Tam went over to his mother, took her roughly by the elbow and steered her towards the door, then signalled with a jerk of his thumb that she should depart. "You just go, Mammy. This is between Dinah and me and I'm gonnae sort it oot Leith-style."

As soon as Mary had left, Tam turned on Dinah. "That wee bastard goes."

Dinah shook her head. "No. He's *my* flesh and blood, just like the others. I could have got rid of him – but know something?" She now looked directly into Tam's eyes and he could see no fear in her gaze. "There isn't a day when I look at him that I'm not glad I didn't."

The belt that Tam had found too big for his waist now

he'd become so thin was still lying where he had left it. Seizing it, he rolled the end once around his hand, stepped forward and lashed out at Dinah.

The first painful lash caught her full on the face and she screamed. The bedroom door flew open and Senga, who had been hushing little Joe to sleep, rushed over to protect her mother.

"Daddy," wailed Senga, struggling to come between him and Dinah, "whatever are you doing?"

By now Dinah was rushing for the door but before she could escape Tam yelled, "You're right! The wee bastard won't be going because after I'm done sorting you out I'm gonnae kill him!"

Dinah hesitated. Tam was now lashing the air with his belt and coming menacingly towards her. Quickly she fled out of the door and began to run round Restalrig Circus. Some of the residents were out and about and they quickly alerted the other neighbours. Soon the spectacle of Dinah being chased round the Circus by Tam wielding a leather belt was holding everybody spellbound.

"That's right, Tam," jeered one old crone who had to remove the clay pipe from her mouth to encourage him. "You gie her the right guid doin' she deserves!" The old woman then cackled but her laughter stuck in her mouth when Mary Glass punched her squarely in the face.

"Oh my goodness," observed Judy Smith. "Did you see that? His mother, his own mother," she emphasised, "standing up for her whoring daughter-in-law that's made her son the laughing-stock of the whole district."

By now Dinah was halfway round the Circus and when she saw that Tam was gaining on her, she kicked off her high-heeled shoes, picked them up and flung them at Tam.

To her amazement, one of the heels caught him in the corner of his eye and, while he tried to stem the blood, she had just enough time to escape, running barefoot over the street. However, instead of taking the opening that would bring her to Restalrig Crescent and into sure safety, she continued to flee round the Circus until Tam's rugby-style tackle brought her down at the large communal area just outside the allotments.

Tam raised the belt again and Dinah rolled herself tightly into a ball with her hands over her head to protect her face. Four lashes rained down upon her as the assembled crowd heckled and urged him on. Tam was about to vent all his five years of anger and frustration on Dinah but this time, as he raised the belt, he felt a fierce punch in his back. Turning around, he was faced by Patsy.

"So you've gone back to the old Leith ways of dealing with a wayward wife, have you? God, are you no just a hero? You ken something, Tam? It must be a guid ten years since I've seen a wife beaten and humiliated in public. And for what? Because, in my Dinah's case, she got a wee bit consolation for all the loneliness she felt ever since you went away?" Tam stood as silent and still as a statue while Patsy went on, after first grabbing the belt from him and hurling it high in the air over into the allotments. "Look, why don't you make a real job of it and go right back to the time when stoning to death was a woman's fate?" she sneered at him.

Dinah meantime had taken the opportunity of her mother's intervention and with the help of Mary, her dear mother-in-law, she managed to stagger to her feet, limp over the road and escape into the safety of her home.

Tam was now breathing heavily and tears were brimming in his eyes but Patsy was not to be deterred. "And tell me this, Tam. Have *you* always been a clean tattie?" Patsy turned to the crowd and bellowed with a broad sweep of her arm to indicate that she included them all, "And you lot can get going. The peep-show's over for the night. And something else . . . Is there even one among the ugly lot of you who could cast the first stone in my Dinah's direction?" She paused before giving a final taunt to the onlookers. "Jealousy's a hellish thing, is it no?"

Patsy then turned to Tam. "You coming home with me or do you mean to entertain your dim-witted audience here with another barbaric pantomime performance?"

When Patsy and Tam entered the house they went immediately into the kitchen where Mary and Etta were attending to Dinah's wounds. "Think that gash on your knee needs a stitch," said Etta as she tried to stem the blood.

"No. I don't want to go to the hospital," protested Dinah. "They would want me to charge him and I don't want that. Even if he has ruined my last pair of nylons!"

"Why not charge him? He blooming well deserves it," argued Etta, who was beginning to wonder what fate awaited her if Harry ever worked it out that her darling son wasn't his!

"I'm not thinking of Tam. I'm thinking about what might happen if the authorities get involved."

"Well, if that's what you want. But along with it will go a bonny scar on your bonny knee."

"Right," said Patsy. "Things have to be settled in here and not outside, making a public spectacle of yourselves." A long silence followed. "So I take it the two of you want to call it a day?" Both Dinah and Tam shook their heads. "So the sticking point is wee Joe?"

Tam nodded. "I want him out of my house."

"And I still say: if he goes, so do I!" retorted Dinah, who had not been cowed in the slightest by the beating.

"Okay," said Patsy, nodding. "How about a compromise – like I take him and you can see him every day?"

"And would that suit Senga?" Dinah replied. "And by the way, where is Senga?"

"She's run away," piped up Elsie, "and she's taken wee Joe with her."

"Took wee Joe with her?" exclaimed Patsy.

"Aye. Put him in his go-cart alang wi' what she thought they'd need."

Dinah forgot all about her wounds, grabbed hold of Elsie and started shaking her. "But why has she gone?"

Elsie's eyes grew wide with fear as she wondered if she was to be the next one to be belted. "Because . . . because . . ." she stammered.

"Because what?" howled her mother, shaking her vehemently.

Tam went over and relaxed Dinah's grip on Elsie. "Look, darling," he said softly. "Don't be afraid . . . Daddy's sorry . . . He was bad – but do tell us why Senga's left home?"

Elsie looked imploringly at her two nodding Grannies before looking back at her father and then uttering reluctantly, "Because she doesn't want you to . . . *kill him*!"

Ten-year-old Elsie, who was desperate to be part of the search, was ordered to stay at home in the care of Tess while everyone else went out to hunt for Senga and Joe. Having made his decision, Tam, who had now taken full charge of the situation, resolved it would be best to break up into pairs. So Tam joined up with his mother Mary. Dinah went with her mother Patsy, and Johnny attached himself to Etta. It was agreed from the start that, since they would be leaving at five o'clock, they would all meet up at seven, whether or not they had managed to trace the missing children.

Elsie had been looking out of the window for half an hour when she called to Tess, "Here's Daddy and Granny Mary coming back but they haven't got Senga and Joe with them." Tess made no reply but joined Elsie at the window. "And look," Elsie cried as she pointed, "there's Mammy and Granny Patsy and they haven't got them either!"

Once assembled in the living room, both exhausted grannies flopped down on chairs and remained speechless. What words could they have spoken that might possibly ease the situation? Two of their grandchildren were missing and it was all because the parents, their own adult children, had lost control of themselves.

Tam too sat down and buried his head in his hands. He was desperate to find a solution but none was forthcoming. Slowly he raised his head. Placing his hands at the back of his neck and entwining his fingers, he gave a long hard look at Dinah. She seemed to have aged ten years in the last few hours. Her lovely face was now taut and drawn, while her body sagged with fatigue. His eyes travelled down to her legs and he winced as he saw the cuts and bruises that had been inflicted by none other than himself! There and then, he vowed that no matter what happened in the future he would never lift his hand to her or his children ever again. Brutality of the kind he had meted out was for barbarians and if he continued to act like one then those who had brutalised him in his captivity would have won.

Dinah was the first to speak. "Right," she said, her voice

115

shaking with emotion, "I think it's now time to get the police involved."

A long silence followed before Patsy replied, "No. It's only half past seven . . . let's give it till nine . . . there's still plenty of daylight."

"You're right, Patsy," agreed Mary. "No polis until it's really necessary. Besides, Johnny and Etta aren't back yet and they might hae found them."

"Will I put the kettle on?" asked Tess, who could think of nothing else to say.

Etta and Johnny had searched in all the most likely places and all the most unlikely places for Senga and Joe – every school playground and every play-park. They even begged the scoutmaster of the 11th Leith troop to let them search the Log Cabin Scout Hall in Craigentinny Road but there was still no sign of the missing pair. From there, they went up to Findlay Gardens and, just as they were approaching Restalrig Crescent, they saw Sam Campbell, a sharp-witted twelve-year-old – who'd had to grow up fast when his father deserted the family and left them destitute – jumping over the railway dyke.

Johnny whistled to alert Sam and Sam stopped and turned. "What's up?" he asked.

Approaching the wall, Johnny jumped up to sit on the dyke while Etta got out her cigarettes and lit up. "Have you seen oor Senga and Joe?" were Johnny's opening words.

Sam shook his head. "Naw. Last time I saw Senga she was reciting in the poetry competition."

"Aye, she won," replied Etta.

"So she should," agreed Sam. "She sure is guid at speaking – even though she's got a bandy leg."

Etta shook her head and Johnny just ignored the remark about Senga and the poetry competition, where she had come first in the whole of Edinburgh, even beating all the posh fee-paying school children. It still rankled that Senga was to be presented with her prize by the Lord Provost up at the City Chambers but that snob of an English teacher at Norton Park School had said it would be better for another pupil – someone else who would create a better impression for the school than Senga with her deformed leg and no school uniform – to receive the accolade, and then Senga could receive it from her. When Senga had come home and told her mother and Granny Patsy what the teacher had proposed, Dinah was incensed and threatened to pull the school down on Miss Strang. Patsy, who very rarely swore, just advised Senga that she should tell Miss Strang to stick the prize up her big arse! And Senga never did accept the prize.

Johnny was about to go and look elsewhere but Etta, who knew Sam very well, said, "Sam. There was another wee spot of trouble . . ."

"About the poetry prize?"

Etta shook her head. "No. About wee Joe – well, Senga's run away and taken him with her."

Johnny snorted through gritted teeth. "Etta! Nobody was to know."

Etta just patted Johnny on the arm. "Look, I've known the Campbell family for years . . . they won't say a word and Sam here will know, if anybody does, where someone would go if they wanted to hide for a while."

Sam became thoughtful. "You know," he said eventually, "if I was doing a runner I think I'd get myself over this dyke so I could get to the Bare Lady . . ."

"Bare Lady?" asked Etta.

"It's a big oak tree just this side of the Eastern General Hospital wall. There's a rope swing there – has been for years – and now the bark is aw worn and white."

"But," argued Etta, with incredulity in her voice, "that's railway property. Trains pass by twice a day."

"Aye," replied Sam, "and the train drivers ken us aw and they just wave to us and blaw us a tune on their whistle."

"Och, but you could be killed," Etta pointed out.

"Naw," replied Sam, "look, there's enough room for three football pitches before the railway line – and just look at the height and breadth of that embankment behind the field."

"Okay," Johnny interjected, "but what guid would it be for Senga to get to the Bare Lady?"

"Well she could hide oot in the gang hut we built just ahint the tree last year."

"But how would she know it was there?"

"Because my eejit sister Carrie took her there last week."

Etta was now climbing up on the dyke.

"Where you going, Etta?" asked Sam.

"To this gang hut, because I just *know* she's there."

"Naw," replied Johnny. "I'll go. You go hame and tell oor Mammy and Daddy where I'm going and where we think Senga and Joe are hiding oot!"

When Etta arrived back at Restalrig Circus she quickly imparted the news that the most likely whereabouts of Senga and Joe could be the gang hut over by the railway line. Now in possession of this possible answer to their problem, they all decided that they would go and find out.

"Well," exclaimed Etta, "if we were to go over the dyke on Restalrig Road, none of you Grannies would make it – in fact, even if we went round and climbed over the Restalrig Crescent way it's going to be hard going," she continued, failing to explain how she knew that.

Undeterred, everyone was determined to go where Senga was supposed to be holed up.

The residents of Restalrig Crescent were treated to a truly unique spectacle as they witnessed the heaving of the grannies, especially of overweight Patsy, up onto the railway wall and then being unceremoniously pushed over the other side. After that, they were amused to see everyone else follow, even Dinah – who had sensibly removed her high heels.

Once over the wall, Etta directed them along the well-worn path at the top of the embankment. All those who had never been there before were astonished that, once past the sand pit, they were faced with a panoramic view of lush green pasture bordered by yet another embankment. At the end of the small green glen and looking towards the top of the embankment, they saw the trees – tall majestic trees that looked as if they had stood there since time began. To reach the small glen, however, they had to climb down the first embankment. As was to be expected, Patsy and Mary held on to each other but they inevitably lost their footing and rolled together to the bottom.

Once everyone was down the hill, Tam, followed by Tess, Elsie and Dinah, raced ahead until Patsy, who was helping Mary to her feet, shouted, "Wait for us. We're family too!"

The group now changed from running to walking until the two grannies finally caught up.

"Where's this gang hut now?" asked a breathless Patsy.

"Up there somewhere . . . I think," came Etta's none-too-confident reply.

"You mean we've got to climb up that blooming mountain?" moaned Mary as she surveyed what looked to her like another Arthur's Seat.

Etta nodded and they began to climb but nearly stopped when they heard a noise of an approaching train. "Quick," shouted Etta. "Lie down in the long grass."

"Why?" asked Dinah.

"Because it's an offence to be here. It's railway property and you could end up having to pay a fine . . . or worse."

All managed to get down into the grass except Patsy but when the train passed the driver gave her a wave, a toot on his hooter and then hollered, "Nice night for a stroll."

Patsy waved back and replied, "Sure is. I've lost my dog and I'm just looking for him."

By dint of pulling and pushing the two grannies, they all eventually arrived, none the worse, at the top of the steep brae. Then Tam hesitated. He just wasn't certain which way to go until Etta pointed to the Bare Lady and said, "I think it'll be somewhere just beyond that tree."

Etta was right and soon they were all gathered at the entrance to a makeshift gang hut.

"You in there, Johnny?" shouted Tam. The sack curtain that was acting as a door was pulled aside and then Sam, followed by Johnny, crawled out. "Senga and Joe in there too?"

"Aye, Mr Glass," replied Sam, "but they're no coming oot until proper terms, that I'll negotiate, hae been agreed."

Along with Dinah, Tam, who wondered who this young

120

upstart of a laddie was and what right he had to arbitrate, went to push past Sam who held up a warning hand. "Did ye no hear what I said? Negotiations first."

"What blinking negotiations? We want them hame and that's all there is tae it," fumed Mary. "Noo, get oot of my way, you bloody naebody!"

"Language! Language! Mind yer language – there's a wee laddie in there!" warned Sam as he pointed his finger at Mary.

"Okay," Tam conceded. "Could Dinah and me sit doon with you and Senga and work something oot?"

Sam sniffed and drew in his cheeks. "Aye, just ye twa, because that's aw there's room for, onyway."

Tam and Dinah entered the gang hut and, peering into the gloom, saw Senga sitting on an old carpet holding Joe on her knee. Relief seeped into them both. In fact, the whole scene looked so absurd that Dinah found herself having to choke back her laughter.

"Now," began Sam, "Senga here has certain conditions that hae to be met afore she leaves this place o' sanctuary."

"Sanctuary!" exclaimed Tam, looking around the squalid structure.

"Aye. Number one is that naebody is to kill wee Joe here."

"That was just an expression uttered in time of stress," defended Tam diplomatically.

"And twa, he's to stay at Restalrig Circus, where Senga promises she'll look after him."

"I agree to no killing him but I think it wuid be best if he stayed with Granny Patsy."

Senga shook her head.

"If that's yer last word," Sam spat, "then aw I've got to

say is that we'll adjourn this meeting until tomorrow when, nae doot, ye'll hae changed yer mind."

Tam now turned and spoke directly to Senga. "So if I don't let him stay at Restalrig Circus, you won't come home?" Senga nodded. Tam pleaded, "But why?"

"Because I love him and if he'd been a bran scone that was a bit mair fired than the others you'd aw hae been fighting who was gonnae hae it."

Tam tried hard not to laugh at her simple reasoning. "Look," he said. "All I want is for us all to be family again but he's not mine – not my own flesh and blood."

"But he cuid be," interrupted Sam. "Aw ye need ti dae is adopt him and he'd be a right bargain 'cause, believe me (and I ken sic things) he'll be a richt braw wee fitballer yin day. Just loves to kick a baw so he does."

Sam bent over and took Senga's hand and squeezed it. She felt a surge of love and admiration for him race through her – feelings that would never leave her. But she thought, "Why would he ever look at me? He's handsome and brave and I'm more than a year older than him and just plain and stupid."

Tam looked at Senga and Sam. He knew he was beaten and so the terms laid out by Sam were agreed, to everyone's delight – even a third condition that hadn't been negotiated, that they all adjourn to the chippie in Restalrig Road and have their tea. Naturally it would be fish suppers all round!

After that they all went home. Tam suggested that Joe should sleep with Johnny as three girls in one bed was quite enough.

"No," replied Senga, who was still not sure that everything had been worked out to her satisfaction. "He sleeps with me."

Tam shrugged and indicated with a nod of his head that he and Dinah should go to their room.

Senga was the last to retire as she had to wash Joe and then get him ready for bed. When finally she slid beneath the bedcovers, still firmly holding on to Joe, she noticed that Elsie was sitting bolt upright. "Listen," whispered Elsie. "Do you hear that? What's Daddy doing to Mammy now? Should we not go in and save her?"

The thumping of the bedstead against the wall grew in speed and noise and Senga gave a little laugh. "No need to worry, Elsie. I used to hear that noise before Daddy went to war – and know something? The louder the noise and the panting, the better Mammy would sing the next morning."

"Hmm," retorted Tess, lifting her pillow to put it over her head. "Well, if that's the case, after tonight's performance she'll be singing the Hallelujah Chorus in the morning!"

PART TWO

16

Dinah was busying herself in the kitchen. The family would all be home for the special dinner they always had at exactly one o'clock on a Saturday. Hot Scotch pies, sausage rolls and bridies were invariably bought by Senga from Dickson's renowned Home Bakery in North Junction Street. Senga didn't seem to mind the wee detour on her way home from Bond Nine where she worked. How could she deny the weekend treat not only to the family but to herself as well?

The pies, after a little reheating in the oven, were served straight but the sausage rolls and bridies were laid out in the large frying pan and a tin of Heinz beans was poured around them before they too were given a nice gentle warm-up on a gas ring.

This Saturday afternoon, all except Tam had assembled and taken their allotted places at the table, the aroma of the heated delicacies only adding to everyone's pangs of hunger.

"Can we no start noo?" asked Johnny, who was anxious to be fed immediately. "I've got a gemme at two o'clock."

"We're waiting for your Daddy. And by the way, since the two of you work in the shipyards thegither, why did he no come up the road with you?"

"We just got oot the gate and that guy . . ."

"What guy?"

"Och, let me finish, Mammy, before you butt in."

Dinah was now over at the cooker giving the frying pan

a good shoogle. "Blast! The beans are drying up," she huffed, before going on: "You were saying, Johnny?"

"That guy Dad was a prisoner of war with . . ."

"Eddie Gibson?"

"Oh Ma, my stomach thinks ma throat's cut so will you just gie me ma bridie and beans and then I'll be better able to tell ye about the guy."

With a sigh, Dinah started to set out the dinner and handed the first plate to Johnny who smiled before attacking his bridie and beans with such vigour that the sauce dribbled down his chin. After he'd wiped the dripping relish with the back of his right hand he licked that too.

Dinah was about to remind Johnny that he'd still to tell her about the man his Daddy had met when the door opened and in strode Tam. "Where the devil have you been?" Dinah demanded. "I held the dinner back for you. The bairns were nearly eating the table they felt so hungry."

After ruffling Elsie's hair, a smiling Tam took his seat and Dinah placed a plate with two Scotch pies in front of him. Putting Dinah out of her agony, Tam began to answer, while reaching over for the HP Sauce bottle. "Andy Young met me at the yaird gates. Had some information for me."

Flashing her gaze towards to the ceiling, Dinah moaned, "Oh, no! And what does Mr Chips think you should be doing noo?"

"Well," responded Tam, slapping the bottom of the sauce bottle so hard that a large dollop landed on Elsie's plate – which caused Elsie to wail that she didn't like brown sauce and all the more so when it was flung at her.

"Well," began Tam afresh, "Andy says that noo I hae my City and Guilds certificate, he's spoken tae a pal up at the Heriot Watt College – in Chambers Street, ye ken – and he says they'll accept me to dae an ONC in Building Construction."

"And how'll you do that and what'll it do to put bread on this table?" Dinah demanded, rapping the table and giving out a deep sigh of exasperation, which she hoped would signal to Tom that she was utterly fed up with his teacher pal, Andy Young, who kept putting such grandiose ideas into her husband's head!

Tam finished his first pie with obvious relish before answering with a chuckle. "The ONC isn't much by itself but it'll take me on to the HNC which," and he put up his hand to emphasise the next point, "I don't really need to get me into Moray House Teaching Training College but it would stand me in good stead – and get me used to studying forbye." Dinah just sat and shook her head. "Mind you," continued Tam, "the other thing is that while I'm getting on with the qualifications at the Heriot Watt, I'll be able to keep the day job and go to evening classes three nights a week."

Dinah realised she would need to try another tactic so she wheedled, "But Tam, won't working all day and all this studying at night school no be too much for you?"

"No," said Tam, taking her hand in his and squeezing it. "Thanks to you, I'm fit enough now. And when I do get my HNC, I'll still be young enough to get on this special Post-War Emergency Training Scheme. Honestly, they're so short of teachers – and they specially want to promote technical subjects to get the economic recovery going – that they've got to do something," he bragged, while giving Dinah a knowing wink.

"But Tam, you're doing well enough, specially with all the overtime. So why . . . ?"

"Look, I'm tired of being a naebody. See, when I graduate

from Moray House, I'll be a professional. Andy says he knows I can do it. And the twa years at Moray House I ken will be the hardest for us because we'll hae to get by on a grant."

"What grant?"

"The one they gie you because I'll be full-time at the college, Dinah. Andy says it will be enough for us to live on."

"Andy says!" yelled Dinah. "And has your blessed Andy tried supporting five bairns for two years on a measly grant?"

"You know fine he's no married. And we've only got Elsie and . . ." Tam swallowed as he always did before adding, "wee Joe to be kept now."

"*I* keep wee Joe," Senga protested. "That's why I work in the Bonds." Senga knew the fact that she was a Bond Lassie irked her father. He'd wanted her to get a *nice* job in an office or at least in a shop like Tess. What Senga had never told anyone was that she'd tried to get a job in the élite Jenners Department Store on Princes Street as a trainee window-dresser but had to give up that dream. They did train you right enough but that was all – no pay, just the prestige of being able to say you'd been trained in Jenners. She had also attended for interview at Binns at the West End of Princes Street and at Patrick Thomson's on the Bridges but the requirement that both legs should be straight prevented her from being offered a position. Senga was also aware that her Daddy, though he tholed Joe, was still not comfortable with him. So, in order to cause wee Joe the minimum of resentment, she'd taken the job offered to her in Bond Nine because the money was good. It paid far in excess of posh jobs!

"Onyway," said Tam, turning to Dinah while popping into his mouth the bread he'd used for mopping up the remaining sauce on his plate. "It'll be four years till we're on the grant and by that time," he gulped, "Joe'll be at school and you can get yourself a wee job." Dinah started to laugh. "What's so amusing about you going out and doing your bit?" spiered Tam.

"Just that, as you've said, you're fighting fit again. So fit actually that it'll be another five years and eight months before I can take on a wee job to keep the home fires burning!"

Tam's mouth sagged. "Are you saying . . . ?"

Dinah smiled, "Five weeks gone – and before you suggest I get rid of it, remember I'm a Catholic."

"You never got rid of *him*," Tam now pointed with his index finger towards wee Joe, "so why would you want tae get rid of my legitimate . . . ?"

"Don't you dare say Joe's no legal," retorted Dinah, going over and placing her hands over the boy's ears. "But to get back to your burning desire – yes, my bonny lad, you can please your pal Andy and go to Moray House – but ask him first how you'll cope with all those sleepless nights that'll be coming up in eight months time!"

When Senga arrived at her Granny Patsy's house, she leant over and tapped on the kitchen window. Immediately the window opened upwards and Patsy stuck her head out. "Nearly ready," she called, looking admiringly at wee Joe in his go-car. "My, you've got him looking just dandy the day. New coat?"

"Yeah, I got it in the Store. Mind you, he'd no clothing coupons left. Daddy wouldn't give him any of his. Says he's got to get a new funeral shirt and suit now he's put on weight."

"Does he think somebody's about to kick the bucket?"

"Other than Granddad Glass . . . ?"

"He'd be a right miss and I don't think so," interrupted Patsy, her voice full of disgust.

"Well, no. Counting granddad, I think everybody else is okay except . . ." Senga hesitated. She wasn't sure if she should tell Granny Patsy about Mammy and Daddy's fall-out. It could be looked upon as being disloyal. But she'd no need to worry for Patsy had taken her head in through the window again and Senga could hear her granny's outside door being banged shut.

As soon as Patsy appeared outside, she pushed Senga away from Joe's go-car and took over pushing the vehicle along the road. "Johnny away on ahead to the football field?"

"Aye. They're playing down on Leith Links – and, Granny," Senga paused for she hated hurting Patsy, "Johnny says even if the ball knocks his head off you've not to run on to the field shouting '*foul*' and then go about lashing out at the laddie that's collided with him!"

Patsy sniffed before explaining, "That was a mistake last week. I never meant to land that Sam Campbell a shot."

"Oh, so you forgot he plays on the same side as Johnny?"

"Sort of. But you see, when I saw our Johnny falling over him I thought he'd deliberately flung himself down on the ground. How was I to know he'd been wrong-footed by the other team's inside-right?"

Senga smiled. She never could stay angry for long with Granny Patsy. She knew that when Granny Patsy did things like smack Sam Campbell it was because she was so besotted with her grandchildren. She was just wondering what life would have been like without her when Patsy stopped pushing the go-car and asked, "You were saying everybody was all right except . . . except who?"

A long silence followed but, as Patsy made no attempt to move on, Senga resolved to tell her what she would find out anyway. "Granny Patsy," she said, "now this is secret. *Very* secret." Patsy crossed herself to acknowledge she was to tell no one what Senga was about to impart. "Well, Daddy's been listening to Andy Young again."

"So what?" remarked Patsy. "He always gives him good advice. Look how he and that Fred guy got him through the war – and not only that, he taught him to read and write."

"That's the problem," explained Senga. "Now he can read and write, he wants to be a teacher."

"How could he be that? He's only a joiner."

"Yeah, but if he goes to night school at the Heriot Watt he could do studying and exams and then go on to teacher-training at Moray House College."

"Hmmm," Patsy half sang. "Good for him. And that wouldnae half cheer up his mammy."

"But that's not all . . ." Senga paused. "He also wants Johnny to go with him."

"Johnny?"

"Aye, he thinks Johnny should be trying to better himself and it would get him paid his worth."

"You mean he'd be paid more than your Dad?"

"Naw, Granny, he wouldn't be paid more that way but he *would* be able to work the hale thirty years or so to get a full pension. Daddy'll be forty-three when he qualifies so he'll only get a wee pension."

"Aye," agreed Patsy, as she moved on. "But it would at least be a pension. Maist of us hae to depend on the State and it's in a right state, is it no?"

"Here, would you look at that?" shouted Senga, as they neared the playing fields. "The game's started and oh, oh, oh!"

"Is that Sam Campbell scoring again?" commented Patsy to Senga, who was now blushing and gasping. "Know something, Senga? He always seems to have that red face effect on you. Do you fancy him or something?"

Shaking her head vehemently, Senga exclaimed, "Me fancy him, Granny? Don't you know he's a whole thirteen months, two weeks and three days younger than I am?"

"Oh, I see. So you don't want to be caught cradle-snatching?"

Refusing to discuss her secret feelings for Sam Campbell, even with her Granny Patsy, Senga decided on a quick change of subject. "Here, Granny," she simpered, "do you think if I took wee Joe to the barber's he could cut away most of these lovely black corkscrew curls that seem to annoy Daddy so much?"

"Well, you could try, but know something? Joe having his hair straightened won't stop you having a crush on bonny, tall, curly-headed Sam Campbell!"

17

"This your first time?" asked the woman in the bed opposite to Dinah.

Dinah reluctantly turned her gaze away from the small delicate bundle she had just given birth to. "No and yes," she replied. "You see, it's the first time I've given birth in a hospital – my other six were born at home."

"Seven in all you've had?" Dinah nodded. "And you look so g-good still," the woman began to stammer. "What I mean is, you dinnae look as if you've been yased as a breeding machine."

Ignoring the woman's remarks, Dinah looked down once again at her precious baby. "Think I'm going to call her Myra after my mother-in-law."

"One o' your other bairns called after your own mammy?"

"No. One Patsy at a time is quite enough for this world."

The woman was now out of bed and came over to sit beside Dinah. "My name's Rosalie O'Donnell. I'm from west of the Shannon."

"Thought you might be Irish with that lovely brogue of yours. I'm Dinah Glass. Think they've put us thegither because we're getting on a bit for having bairns."

Rosalie laughed and her whole face lit up. "This wee soul now," she said, pulling down the baby's shawl to get a better look. "Did she come as much as a surprise as mine did?" Dinah nodded.

"I'm forty, would you believe it? My youngest laddie is

eighteen and here's me . . . Ah well, the milkman's got a lot to answer for."

Dinah looked quizzical but decided not to pursue Rosalie's confession – if it really was one. "I'm thirty-eight but my last wee one, a laddie, is just three. You know, I just don't know what it is about April the first that makes me feel I *have* to give birth!"

The evening visiting session officially allowed no more than two visitors at the bedside, but since no one was willing to be left out of the group that had come to inspect the new member of the Glass family, Dinah had continued to have her whole family crowd round her.

Tam was first to pick up little Myra and his eyes moistened as he held her. "Think she's very like you, darling," he said, looking directly at Dinah.

"Any good news?" Dinah replied.

Tam handed Myra to Patsy who promptly summoned Mary to come over and admire the latest addition. "Any good news, you ask?" he said thoughtfully, taking Dinah's hand in his. "Now, let's see. Would Johnny and me passing our first-year exams at the Heriot Watt count?"

Dinah pulled her hand away from Tam's. "No! But winning the pools would!"

"But you know I'm against gambling, so I don't do the pools," protested Tam.

Dinah was about to make a caustic retort when a drunk and dishevelled man staggered into the ward and lurched his way to Rosalie's bed. "Another wee thon," he lisped. He tried to bend over the bed to kiss his wife but almost fell over. Regaining his balance he then shouted to the whole ward, "Ken what all the boys in the docks thaid?" No one spoke so he went on. "They thaid, they did, that thomeone had had it in for me!"

To which Rosalie replied quietly, with a wink to Dinah, "Didn't believe me, did you? But now you do."

Before anything else could be said, Tam and Johnny had to take their leave of Dinah so as to go to their evening class. Both grandmothers meantime were anxious that the children shouldn't start asking what Rosalie meant so Patsy blurted out, "Here, Dinah, you're never going to believe this – but Mary and me hae joined the Co-op Women's Guild."

Dinah's eyes widened in mock amazement as she replied, "Oh, that's the most exciting thing I've heard since Betty Grable insured her legs for a million dollars."

Patsy well knew that Dinah was being sarcastic and she nudged Mary before going on. "You tell her, Mary. Tell her just where we'll be going with the Guild and who we'll be seeing."

Mary looked warily about the ward and a coy look overtook her before she confided, "Blackpool! And we'll be staying in a Bed and Breakfast!"

"Blackpool? And staying in a Bed and Breakfast!" exclaimed Dinah. "But how on earth can you two – especially you, Mammy, who's always pleading poverty – possibly afford that?"

"Well," continued Mary, relishing her moment of glory, "it's only for the September weekend, Dinah. No for the whole week."

"And," Patsy quickly interrupted, "as we start paying it up from now, not only will it all be paid for before we go, but we'll also hae saved up oor spending money."

"And remember, Patsy," Mary continued, with a deliberate

pause to add to the suspense, "that it also includes oor tickets to see Joseph Locke in the theatre – and in the Winter Gardens, at that. Just imagine it." Mary now looked over to Patsy and grinned. "Little old us going to the Winter Gardens to see all the big stars!"

"Next thing you'll be telling me, Mary, is that you'll be getting a wee perm before you go."

"It's already been booked – and Etta's going to lend me a suitcase."

By the time the September weekend came along, the household in Restalrig Circus had settled down, complete with baby Myra. All that is, except for wee Joe, who couldn't understand why everything wasn't still revolving around himself. "Jealous wee blighter," remarked Tam, who took every opportunity to pick Myra up and nurse her – something he wasn't seen to do with Joe when anybody was about.

Dinah and Senga, lugging the suitcases, escorted the two grannies down to Fire Brigade Street where all the buses were lined up, ready to take the eager passengers to Blackpool for the weekend.

"Which bus are we on?" Mary asked, grabbing hold of Patsy's arm.

"That one. See – there's Ella ticking off everyone from her sheet as they get on."

Mary giggled. "So she is. Quick, Patsy. Let's get aboard so we can get a good seat thegither."

As Patsy and Mary scrambled aboard the bus, Dinah and Senga were left to heave the cases up into the luggage rack.

"You know, Mum, you'd think they were off for a week to Butlins in Ayr the way they're carrying on," remarked

Senga, who was vastly amused that a weekend trip, even if it was to Blackpool, could cause so much excitement.

"Aw well," replied Dinah, who was secretly pleased that the two were off on their own. "You see, they've never really had the wherewithal to go any further than Porty beach, where for thruppence the café will fill your teapot with hot water. So this is all a great adventure – and good luck to them. But know something?" she trilled delightedly and then slipped her arm through Senga's as they both waved furiously when the bus engines roared into life and set off into Great Junction Street. "How do you think we'll keep them down in the farm now when they've seen Blackpool?"

Dinah was still arm-in-arm with Senga as they made their leisurely way home. This intimacy gave Senga – who always felt she was the *saftest* in the family, the only Johnny-raw – the much-needed confidence she usually lacked. For some time she'd been wanting to talk to her mother about confidential matters that were worrying her. "Mammy," she said hesitantly, "ken the lassies in the Bond?" Dinah nodded. "Well they're arranging a night oot for Halloween."

"Oh, that's good. And you should go. Get mixing with lassies your own age instead of always taking wee Joe with you everywhere." Senga bristled but Dinah went on, "Spoil your chances, so he will, because the laddies will be thinking he's yours, and with him being . . ."

Senga, who always turned herself off when anyone commented that her Joe was of mixed race, abruptly interrupted. "They're haeing their tea oot in a chippie first, they are. Then going on to Fairley's Dance . . ."

Now it was Dinah's turn to break in as she pulled her

arm abruptly away from Senga's. "Fairley's Dance Hall in Leith Street?" Senga nodded. "But that's the place where whores pick up the sailors!"

"Mammy, if you'd let me finish. Before the lassies go into Fairley's, their boyfriends are meeting up with them so there'll be nae problems for them . . ." Senga turned and looked straight at her mother. "But as I've no got a boyfriend, and oor Johnny has told me to 'get lost' 'cause he wouldnae be seen dead in the place, I was wondering if it would be out of order to ask a neighbour laddie?"

Dinah sighed. She remembered that she had been just Senga's age, fifteen, when she'd fallen for Tam and how painful it had been when their families had tried to keep them apart. But it had been different for her and Tam because they'd been besotted with each other. In Senga's case, Dinah (who knew her children only too well) was aware that Senga was bewitched by Sam Campbell, who was only going on fourteen. Dinah shook her head. There was just no way a fifteen-year-old naïve lassie and a fourteen-year-old laddie, even if he was as worldly wise as Sam, would be allowed into Fairley's. But more importantly, she didn't want Senga entering that den of iniquity. "Look, Senga darling," she began, "you're just too young for that kind of dance hall. And you shouldn't be throwing yourself at any boy . . . or young man . . ."

"I'm not throwing myself at any laddie. I was just going to ask someone to take me to the dance hall," a tearful Senga protested.

Dinah sighed. She knew she should have handled the situation better. Nevertheless, the most important thing for her was to protect her love-sick daughter from herself. Reluctantly she emphasised, "Forget this Halloween night out, Senga. Maybe in a year or two things will be different."

"How?"

"Well, for a start, you're a cut above Fairley's right now. And in time you just might get enough sense to see that."

18

Tam had a spring in his step as he headed home from the interview at Moray House College. He just couldn't believe that he, who had been quite illiterate at the start of the war, now held a Higher National Certificate in Construction and that it had seen him accepted to start his teacher training at Moray House in August.

He knew Dinah would be pleased, very pleased, but she would pretend that his *vaulting ambition* (as she put it) irked her. But Tam knew it didn't because before every night-class his evening meal (and Johnny's, who was also doing an HNC) would be on the table as soon as they arrived home. She would also make sure that the two of them were out of the door in time to catch the 6.15pm bus.

As Tam turned into Restalrig Circus, six-year-old Joe, who was playing football in the street, saw him and raced across shouting, "Daddy. Daddy! See how I can trap the ball." Joe then kicked the tennis ball he was playing with high into the air and, as it came to land, he flicked it neatly under his left foot.

"Hmm," commented Tam, who had realised that if he was going to be a successful teacher he must treat all his pupils as equals – no matter their race, creed or religion. Having decided this philosophy was the right thing, he accepted he'd best begin with a change of approach at home. For three months now, he'd spent time building up a positive relationship with his adopted son. For Joe's part, he appeared not to notice any difference in Tam's dealings with him. In the past, even when Tam's rejection of him was obvious to everyone else, the wee lad had been oblivious and had given Tam all the love and respect that a doting son could give a father. Joe now kicked the ball up once more and again trapped it with his left foot when it landed. "You know, son," Tam continued, ruffling Joe's curly dark pow, "you should keep practising with that left foot. Not many have that gift."

Dinah's opening the window and calling, "Joe, your tea's oot," brought a smile to Tam's face.

"Now," he said, grasping Joe's hand and steering him indoors, "did you ever hear, anywhere else, such a summons spoken in such wonderfully dulcet tones?"

The atmosphere in the house was electric. Celebrations were the order of the day and Dinah had prepared a special meal – even baking a cake, icing it and putting a candle on it.

Entering the house, Tam made a grab for Dinah and whirled her around. "Gosh!" she said once he had put her down. "Whatever was that in aid of?"

"Me! Me! Being accepted to train to be a *sir*!" Tam chortled. "But," he continued, "you already knew that because you've got the celebration tea ready."

Dinah looked aghast but did manage to reply, "Well, of course you being accepted for Moray House and us looking forward to two years in the grubber has to be marked." She paused before going on. "But there's also Tess getting engaged and . . ."

Tam puffed and threw himself down on a chair. "I completely forgot that my Tess said she was going to get hitched to that time-and-motion-study bloke."

143

"He came to our Bond last week. Just sits and watches what you do and then scribbles away on his notepad," confided Senga. "And you know what happens then?" Everyone shook their heads. "Then I'll tell you – two days later, the way things have been done for years have to change."

"Like what?" asked Elsie.

Senga took some time to answer. "Now, you're never going to believe this," she said, "but we now have to go for a pee in our *break time*. And if we ask to go too often outside that time, we have to produce a line from our doctor saying we've got cystitis, whatever that is, or in Mary Davidson's case a weak bladder." Senga sighed before going on. "And know this? The worry of not being able to go when we want has us all needing to go all the time. There's never a time around our table when someone hasnae got their hand up. Jenny Stock, oor forewoman, says if we're all still dribbling away the morn, then she's gonnae put us aw back into nappies!"

Before anyone else could speak, the door opened and in flounced Tess, flashing her engagement ring and announcing, "Been a change of plan, Senga. Rupert thinks you should meet the guy who's going to be our best man." Flashing her ring for a second time, she hesitated as everyone waited expectantly. "And, as he's here tonight, my Rupert's going to treat us all to a meal at the . . . Wee Windaes!"

"The Wee Windaes in the High Street?" Tess nodded and again displayed her ring ostentatiously. "Oh, but one of the lassies in the Bond went there on her wedding day. Just four of them that was and she had something called Chicken Maryland."

"In the name of heavens! What kind of thing is that?" asked Dinah as she went through into the kitchen.

Senga dutifully followed her mother and everyone else flocked behind her. "Well, it's chicken breast and a banana, would you believe it – now that you can get them again – all coated in batter, just like a fish, with a piece of bacon and then . . ."

"Oh for heaven's sake, Senga, we accept you know how it's cooked but do get a move on. Honestly, at the rate you're going over a bit of chicken I'll be making tomorrow's porridge afore you're finished."

"Anyway, Senga," Tess butted in, "if you're going to order Chicken Maryland, you can't have soup first. But what's much more important is what you're going to wear. You want to make as good an impression as you can."

Senga's face lit up. "My new skirt. See that Christian Dior? He does such great things for lassies like me."

"Right enough," smirked Tess, "in his New Look nobody will notice your . . ."

Dinah knew Tess was about to say "bandy leg" so she raised her voice and asked, "Now that Tess and Senga are going to a posh restaurant, is there anybody here going to eat this chopped pork, Heinz vegetable salad and chips?"

By now Granny Patsy had come in and exclaimed, "Chopped pork and no Spam? Things really are looking up."

"Aye, Mammy, chopped pork it is and not only that – I asked the grocer to open a new tin so it's a lot fresher than you are."

"Here, Patsy," shouted Tam, who didn't like when Dinah insulted her mother, "seeing there was enough for everyone and now two aren't going to eat with us, how about you joining us?"

"Try stopping her!" muttered Dinah under her breath.

Patsy immediately took off her coat, hung it up behind the door and sat down at the table. "Now, I'm not wanting to be depriving you lot, but seeing you insist," she remarked complacently, lifting a knife and fork. "I just cannae bear to see good food going to waste – especially as I haven't had chopped pork for such a long time."

On their arrival at the Wee Windaes, Tess and Senga were surprised to discover that Rupert and his best-man-to-be weren't there. "I think there's a table booked in a Mr Rupert Harrison's name?" Tess advised the waitress who was looking at her dubiously.

"Ah yes," replied the girl. "May I take your coats? Your table is over there in the corner."

Tess and Senga had been seated perusing the menu for fully five minutes when a breathless Rupert arrived with another out-of-breath gentleman. "Sorry we're late," said Rupert, sitting down opposite Tess. "And this here is my late cousin, Bert Crosby, whom everybody calls Bing."

Senga's first thoughts about Bing were that he needed someone to straighten his tie. His sports jacket, moreover, looked like a hand-me-down that was at least two sizes too big for him, while his hair – well, Senga didn't think any hairdresser would admit to having had their scissors near him. For all that, there was just something so engaging about him – unlike Rupert, who always wore a long overcoat and looked as if he'd been cut off at the knees. Bing, on the other hand, was tall and muscular, exuding an attractive odour of masculinity.

"You a time-and-motion guy like Rupert here?" Senga asked.

"No," replied Rupert curtly. "If he was, we'd have

been dead on time. Wasting time should be a criminal offence."

Senga smiled at Bing. She thought that her sister getting herself hitched to a blooming bore like Rupert ought to be a criminal offence. To her relief, Bing smiled back at her and, picking up the menu, asked, "Have you been here before?" Senga shook her head. "The lads in the crematorium where I work all said I would definitely have to try the Chicken Maryland."

Senga started to laugh uproariously at this and Bing's face blushed beetroot-red. "You laughing because you think I'm in a dead-end job? Well, let me tell you that no one who has ever come to the crematorium has ever complained about my work."

"No, no!" protested Senga, who was still giggling. "It was just that before we left home I told my family about the girls in the Bond, where I work, saying the same thing about the Chicken Maryland."

"Oh, you work in the Bond office?"

"No, Bing, I work in the bottling plant. And no one who has ever tasted Bond Nine whisky has ever said our product isn't anything but good. In fact, after two or three snifters they're, like your customers, speechless!"

Summoning the waitress with a wave of his hand, Rupert said. "Let's order, but . . ."

"It's all right, Rupert, darling, Senga knows that Chicken Maryland is expensive and so she's not going to order any soup!"

Senga and Bing were meandering their way home behind Tess and Rupert. "Was that your first time at that restaurant?"

Giving Bing a sideways glance, Senga pondered before answering. "If I was being truthful, it's the first time I've been in *any* restaurant. You see, I have to contribute to my wee brother Joe's upkeep, so there's not much left for going to fancy places."

"Yeah. Rupert was saying Joe wasn't really one of you, with him being . . ."

Senga stopped abruptly. "Being what?" she snapped.

"I m-meant no offence," Bing stammered. "It was just that Rupert said . . ."

Interrupting again, Senga retorted, "Rupert should mind his own business and I can assure you that our Joe, unlike your Rupert, wouldn't say to anyone, 'You won't be wanting coffee and we'll save the money on bus fares by walking home.'" Senga thought about what she'd just said and the sheer absurdity of it made her cover her mouth to control the laughter. "Sorry," she mumbled. "No way would our wee lad of six be in a restaurant ordering coffee or thinking of saving money by walking. All he thinks about is football."

Bing too was laughing. "Okay, you don't want to tell me who he belongs to and that's fine by me."

"He belongs to us. When Daddy came home at the end of the war he adopted him and so did the rest of us."

The following Saturday, Senga and Joe pitched up to see Johnny playing in his last game for the Edina Hearts. Johnny had mixed feelings about the match. He wasn't sure if being called up to do his National Service was quite what he wanted to be doing. And as for Edina Hearts – well, he was a good player but not a star like Sam Campbell. Sam looked as if he belonged on the football pitch and the recent successes of Edina Hearts were all due to him. The galling thing for Johnny was that Sam was three years younger than him and yet was so skilled you'd think he was the senior of the two.

Senga and Joe had only just arrived when Joe ran on to the field and was kicking the ball that was being used for a warm-up before the match when a lad shouted, "Here, missus, keep your brat under control. Oor fitbaw gemmes are serious stuff!"

Running on to the pitch to grab hold of Joe, Senga stumbled and, trying to regain her balance, fell backwards and could do nothing else but look up at the sky and admire the fluffy clouds.

"Enjoy your trip?" asked the familiar voice of Sam Campbell, holding out his hand to help her to her feet.

Blushing, Senga shook her head and then noticed that Sam had been joined by the referee who was wondering whatever was going on. "This here," informed Sam, "is Johnny Glass's sister. Can't remember her name but it doesn't matter because I just call her Crystal. Have done that for years."

"You call her Crystal. But why?" demanded the referee, retrieving the ball from Joe.

Sam thought for a minute. "Don't really know why. But I think it's because I've known her all my life and her surname's Glass. But don't you think she's looks nicer and sparkles much better than glass?" The man stayed non-committal but a sly smile spread across his face.

Senga felt her whole body tingle with delight. And Sam's statement put straight out of her head any thought of the invitation for a date she'd had from Bing Crosby. That Sam Campbell called her Crystal because she sparkled for him was all that occupied her mind!

19

Tess's wedding reception *had* to be posh – she simply had to be one up on her best friend, Jean. So a boiled ham tea in her parents' living room was not on. Anyhow, Granny Patsy, who stayed next door to the YMCA in Restalrig Road, and never complained about the continual noise and nuisance, solved the problem by approaching them about hiring the hall. They readily agreed that Tess's reception could be held there, provided it would be on a Saturday night, when the hall was available for functions.

Dinah, who was now battling a persistent and wearisome cough, said she was at a loss to understand what difference there was between having a boiled ham tea in the family home and eating it at the YMCA? After all, the catering was still having to be done by herself – and then the meal would need to be transported to the hall.

The only plus about the wedding, where they had even had to send out written invitations, was that, despite having expected life to be very tough living on a grant, it didn't turn out so bad for the couple. Not bad at all in fact! And with Dinah working the twilight shift at Duncan's chocolate factory, they could even afford to pay for the blooming reception. In addition, Tam (or Tom as all his college mates called him) was quite a different man now. He sensed he had a real purpose in life, knowing that in another year he would be a fully qualified teacher – a professional – and able to provide very adequately for his family. He was even toying with the idea that, once qualified, he might be able to get a mortgage and move the family down Restalrig Road into a much larger private house – but this was a thought he kept strictly to himself. The prospect of a mortgage would put the fear of death into Dinah.

After the ceremony, the family all grouped together outside St John's East Parish Church to have their photographs taken. Tess, her father thought, made a beautiful bride. As for the groom, Tam still couldn't warm to him. Even last week, when he came along to the showing of presents, Rupert had to demonstrate yet again how clever he was. This time his target was Dinah and she felt humiliated when he announced to the gathering just how much time and money she wasted every day. "Mrs Glass," he sneered patronisingly, "have you ever thought about how much those cigarettes cost that you light up every half hour or so? And how much time you waste sitting down to have a puff, not to mention having to rest because of your cough?"

Rupert had met Granny Patsy only once before and was decidedly taken aback when she curtly retorted, "I don't know how to say this politely, but have *you* ever thought how much time *you* waste by letting your belly rumble afore you've put your brain into gear?"

The assembly all laughed but luckily the photographer defused the situation by calling for Dinah and Tess to pose together. Tam, who was still chuckling inwardly, took a step back to admire his wife and daughter. Tears welled up in his eyes as he looked at them. They were his pride and joy. However, as he gazed at Dinah, who was now looking more beautiful and entrancing than ever, he felt a strange sense of dread come over him. Was it just that he had to accept that his children were all growing up and would all too soon be flying the nest? Maybe his dislike of Rupert had made him particularly apprehensive; all he could hope for here was that his other children would marry people he could get on with – and admire. As his feeling of foreboding deepened, he just hoped it was not the prelude to something more sinister.

The reception went well. Everyone complimented Dinah on producing such succulent steak pies followed by trifles, only one of which had been dropped on the floor by Tam's brother, Archie. The mess was cleared up by the time the accordion player arrived and the dancing began.

The bride and groom had departed but the party was still in full swing when Tam had to announce it was now eleven-thirty and since tomorrow was the Sabbath the festivities had to be brought swiftly to an end.

Crystal (having officially adopted her beloved nickname) had declined Bing's offer to walk her home. She truly did like him but felt she didn't wish to get into a serious relationship – well, not right now, but maybe one day . . . Well, didn't everyone deserve to have a dream? And, who knows, dreams just might come true.

She was walking alone down Restalrig Road when she saw a group of youths who seemed to be harassing someone. When she drew level, she became aware that the person being bullied was her Uncle Archie. Poor Archie, who they said was "slow", had his hands covering his head and was begging the thugs to leave him alone.

"Right!" Crystal shouted, bursting into the group. "You just leave him alone! You're a pack of yellow-livered cowards."

"Says who?" came the mocking reply from the leader of the gang.

"Says me," Crystal defiantly replied.

"And what are you going to do?" sneered the youth, going over and starting to poke Crystal in the shoulder.

"Her? Nothing. But me, plenty if you don't get your hands off her," a voice rang out.

Crystal sagged with relief. She knew that voice so well and so did the gang, who began to disperse and saunter off.

"Thank you, Sam," said a tearful Crystal, as she helped her uncle to his feet. "They're just scum. My poor uncle doesn't bother anyone. Just goes to his work every day. And he did so enjoy himself at the wedding."

"Come on now," said Sam, linking his arm through Archie's. "We'll just walk you home and then I'll see . . ." Sam had forgotten Senga's name again so he just continued with ". . . see Crystal home."

"Funny," mumbled Archie as they set off, "hoo everybody caws her Crystal noo instead of Senga. Wonder wha changed her name?"

Crystal didn't volunteer an explanation but she did begin to realise why she'd resisted Bing's attentions yet again. Every time she was beginning to weaken and think about saying yes to a date with Bing, Sam Campbell seemed to turn up.

20

There was a gentle knock on the outside door before it opened and in walked Etta.

"You must be psychic," exclaimed Dinah as she dashed into the bedroom and came back carrying a large carrier bag from which she took a dress, a jacket and then a hat.

"Another wedding in the family?" asked Etta, feeling the glossy fabric of the dress.

"No," Dinah retorted. "Remember last week I told you that Tam's graduating this Friday and as me and his mother Mary are both going to see him," she giggled, "getting . . . *capped*, I thought I'd splash out and go to the do all dressed to kill!"

Etta smiled. "You'll sure knock all the fuddy-duddies dead with that outfit!"

"Here! Did I tell you he's got the job at David Kilpatrick's as a Technical teacher, starting in August?"

"David Kilpatrick's? Now is that no where his prisoner of war pal's the deputy head?"

Dinah snorted before replying, "Yes. But my Tam got the job on his own merits. Hasn't he just been told he's top student of the year? And would you believe, he's getting presented with a medal by Moray House College to prove it. I'm really pleased about that so I can show it to folk like you, Etta, who dinnae really believe it!"

"Here, dinnae get so shirty. I was just saying."

"Sorry. But here! Is there something on your mind?"

"What makes you think that?"

"Just that you've been round at least five times in the last three days and you always seem to be wanting to say something important and then you just gossip."

A long silence followed which allowed Dinah to put on her new hat and stand back awaiting Etta's approval – which didn't come. However, Etta did manage to stammer, "Och, Dinah, it's that blooming man of mine, Harry, blackmailing Jacob again. You know how he hasn't done a hand's turn since he was demobbed at the end of the war. My little indiscretion that resulted in our Bill's arrival gave him the excuse never to look for work. Lazy sod, so he is." Etta was now becoming quite emotional. "He says that if Jacob doesn't give him two hundred pounds so he can emigrate to Australia – he'll put an advert in the *Evening News* saying . . ." Etta looked about the room to make sure she and Dinah were alone before she whispered, "that our wee lad's no his and that his father is . . ."

Dinah took off her hat, sat down on the settee and patted it, motioning to Etta to come and sit with her. "I know two hundred pounds is a lot of money but would it not be cheap at the price if he went to Australia and . . . got lost?"

"Hmm," Etta snorted. "Last year he stung Jacob for fifty pounds – said he'd been offered a job in Spain picking oranges!"

"Picking oranges?"

"Aye, and we should have known it was a con because he's aye so befuddled by the booze we have to provide that he cannae even pick his nose – never mind oranges."

"What a bugger." Dinah sat thoughtfully for a minute before tapping Etta's hand and saying, "How about you call his bluff and say, okay, but make it clear you'll buy the boat ticket and then you and I can see him aboard and no leave Liverpool docks until his ship sails?"

Sighing, Etta replied, "Wish it was as easy at that." She then changed the subject by asking, "But here, know how you were telling me you and Tam had been looking at the end-terraced villa down in Restalrig Road? So what's the latest?"

Dinah grinned and hunched her shoulders in delight. "We've got a mortgage from the Halifax Building Society – them up in George Street. See, when you're a professional it's easier to get a mortgage, whether you can pay or no."

"So I take it the offer's in?"

"Aye, we'll ken next Friday."

"Good for you."

"To be truthful, I'm a wee bit scared of that mortgage thing. But we had to do something. This wee hoose here has been great and I do love it, but with Johnny getting demobbed and coming home in the next two weeks and Joe needing a bed all to himself because he lies asleep scoring goals all night . . . As for Crystal – well, there's no sign of her being taken off our hands. And Elsie's now starting to work . . . did I tell you she's got a start at William Nimmo's, the big Leith printers, as a trainee layer-on – and as she's clever, she's also going to be copy-holder!" Dinah, so proud of Elsie's achievement, savoured the moment before saying, "Then there's our baby, Myra, now turning five and if that's no enough to be over-crowding us, now that Tam's dad, Jack, has done the decent thing at last and got to hell out of oor road . . ."

"Do you really think there would be no chance of him getting into heaven? I mean, did he no repent afore he went?" enquired Etta, who was still a gentle creature at heart and didn't like the thought of anyone, even Jack Glass or her Harry (when he did go), roasting in a fire for ever.

"No repent? Look, Etta, he dropped down deid but even if he'd been given two years' warning it still wouldnae hae been time enough for him to confess aw his sins."

"Okay. But what difference will his going make to you?"

"Well, Tam's now saying, that if anything happens to his mother, then Archie will be coming to bide with us," said Dinah, with a sigh.

"But he's a canny cratur, Dinah. He'll no cause you any bother. You wouldnae want him having to go to the Model Lodging House, would you?" Etta argued.

"Suppose not. And by the looks of Mary, since she and my Mammy are forever going on Mystery Drives and weekends away to Blackpool, she might well go on forever."

"Talking of that, is it true that when you all got down to the crematorium, Mary asked that lad, Bing, who's nuts about Crystal, to make sure and put an extra shovelful on, specially for Jack?"

"No," laughed Dinah, "but right after the service, we did go and hae oor tea oot in Smith's Tea Rooms on the corner of Morton Street and Duke Street and then we went up to the Empire Theatre. Lucky we were, getting the last tickets for Vera Lynn's show. Great singer she is. Mind you, Mary thought that her singing 'We'll Meet Again' was a bit depressing!"

Etta too was now laughing but when Crystal came in the smile died on both their faces. "What is it, hen?" asked Dinah. "What's wrong?"

"Oh, Mammy, Sam Campbell's going off to do his

National Service and when he comes back he'll be joining the polis!"

"Mmm," uttered Etta, taking out a packet of cigarettes and handing one to Dinah while lighting another for herself. "There's a plus in everything?"

"And what plus is in it for me when he'll probably be *killed*?" whimpered Crystal.

"Just that you might see sense and get courting that lad at the crematorium."

By now Dinah had her cigarette half-smoked but on the next draw she started to cough violently. "Time you saw about that cough, my lady," advised Etta, who had also begun to clear her own throat.

"Suppose I should," spluttered Dinah. "But this bark's because ... I just can't stop laughing! Oh Etta, d'you not think that if a lad's been with the dead all day long he should be looking for someone a bit more cheerier than my Crystal?"

21

The middle-aged man ran his hands over his worn and dusty boiler-suit before placing his right palm on the recently painted wrought-iron gate while grabbing his chin with the left. He desperately wanted to open the gate and walk up the path that led to the rather imposing (as he saw it) semi-detached villa – but he somehow lacked the courage. Luck was on his side, however, for without warning the half-glass door of the house was thrown open wide and Etta called out, "You going to stand there all day, Archie?"

Still hesitant, Archie opened the gate and began to creep up the path, again running his hands over his overalls. "Is Dinah in?" he asked. Etta nodded. "Do you think she'll want me to go round to the back door seeing I've still got my working claithes on?"

"For heaven's sake, Archie, don't be so daft."

His face turning crimson, Archie half-hung his head before piteously retorting, "I'm no daft." He paused before adding, "I work the hale time. And take my wages hame to my Mammy every week."

Etta winced before skipping down the path to take Archie by the arm and steer him indoors. "I know you're no daft. Sorry. It's me that's daft saying a thing like that. But Archie, there's no way that Dinah would have you going to the back door. You're family and we all love you."

Dinah was in the kitchen, which was next to the back living-room, and she called out, "Here, Etta, did you say Archie boy was coming in?"

159

"Aye, and here he is. Meaning to go round to the back door, he was. Huh!"

Emerging from the kitchen, Dinah dried her hands on a towel. "Why would you want to do that? But here! Why aren't you at work?"

"Sent hame," Archie replied, going over to Dinah and pointing a finger towards his swollen cheek. "Look. Mammy said if my rotten tooth was to bother me again I was to come round to you."

Peering into Archie's mouth Dinah could see the problem. "Need to get you to a dentist, Archie," she announced, glancing up at the clock and wondering if she could get him to one and be home in time for Joe and Myra coming out of school.

Archie immediately backed away from her, shouting, "Naw, naw. You're no taking me down to that roughie in Bonnington Road."

"What roughie is he talking about?"

"Och, Etta, don't tell me you've never heard about Miss Cowie. She's real rough and a true sadist. Hasnae heard of anaesthetics, straps you into the chair and then throws her leg up on your chest to haud you down afore hauling your tooth out – and often enough she pulls the wrong yin!"

Archie had collapsed on a chair and his pallor was a mixture of white and blue. "I'm no going there. I'm no going there. I was ta'en tae her when I was just five . . . and I've never been back. Wouldnae even go to the school dentist down in Links Place efter that Miss Cowie scared me so much. Blood everywhere, so there was. And she didnae even get my tooth oot."

"But if she didn't pull your tooth out, where did all the blood come from?" enquired Etta.

"My nose," replied Archie. "Because when she saw me running for the door she socked me a shot."

"Okay, okay. Just calm down, Archie. There's no use taking you to Miss Cowie – because she's deid and I havnae the time to do a séance. So we'll just skip down the road to my dentist in Vanburgh Place." Archie shook his head. "Look, son," Dinah went on, "I promise you Mr Wilson will put you right to sleep and when it's all over your tooth will be out and the pain gone." Archie shook his head again. "You just cannae go on with the agony, Archie. And know something? Rabbie Burns didnae call it 'the hell o' aw diseases' for nothing. You've been real brave this far, but let's put an end to it."

"Wish Mammy hadnae gone off on that Mystery Tour to North Berwick."

Dinah thought, "So do I. And why did they always say they were off on a Mystery Tour when they knew full well, before they left, that they would be landing up just where they wanted to be – in North Berwick for the mandatory fish tea followed by some Luca's ice cream."

Archie winced again and gently rubbed his cheek. "Promise I'll feel nothing?" Dinah nodded reassuringly.

Dinah and Etta waited anxiously in the waiting room and both heaved a sigh of relief when Mr Wilson came out and said he had removed two additional teeth that would have caused bother in the next wee while and that he'd also cleaned up Archie's mouth. He hesitated briefly before adding that since he was having difficulty rousing Archie, he'd sent for Dr Hannah just to give him the once-over.

Mr Wilson had just imparted this news when Dr Hannah

arrived, smiling to Dinah and Etta, both of whom were patients of his. He promptly disappeared into the surgery and when he reappeared, physically assisting a revived Archie, both women tangibly felt released from the sense of terror that had engulfed them. With shaking hands, Dinah took out her cigarettes and lit up one but was immediately overtaken by a fit of coughing.

"Here. That cough sounds as if it's coming from the soles of your boots, Mrs Glass," observed Mr Wilson.

Dr Hannah took the cigarette from Dinah and stubbed it out before saying, "I think it's about time you came down to see me about your chest."

"I did come down last week but there were twenty people waiting in your surgery. And after being told there were only you and young Dr Milne on duty, I came away. Just couldn't wait well over an hour – so I thought, why bother?"

"Believe you me, it's more than important that you *do* bother. So I'll expect to see you tomorrow!"

Dinah wanted to go on with her explanation but the doctor's abrupt departure put an end to that.

By the time Dinah and Etta had helped Archie up the road, the children were home from school. However they needn't have worried as Tess had already arrived, and, knowing how hungry children always were when they came in from school, she had spread some jam on bread. Not only was that a real delicacy for Joe and Myra, it was also a pleasure for Etta's son, Bill, who always came first into the Glass household for a jammy piece before returning to his own home.

Tess's face was full of concern when she looked at her

162

uncle's face, so drawn and sickly. "Whatever happened?" she gasped.

"Got three teeth out, he did," Dinah replied. "But once he's had a good sleep he'll be right as rain." Turning to Archie, she ordered, "Now, take yourself upstairs and get into the bed in the back room and no one will bother you. And you'll be sleeping here all night."

"But will Mammy no be worried when she gets hame and I'm no in my ain bed?"

"No. I'll get one of the bairns to run up with a note and put it in the letterbox."

Archie nodded. "Thanks, Dinah. You're a real swell. I just dinnae feel I'd want to be all on my ain the noo."

Once Archie had taken his leave and Etta had departed with Bill, Tess looked at her mother. "Mam," she said, biting on her lip, "I'm going to have a baby."

"A baby!" exclaimed Dinah. "Oh, great. I just love babies, so I do. And your grannies will be cock-a-hoop. When's it due?"

"June next year. And Rupert says the added bonus is that – what with him getting me . . ." Tess laughed and patted her stomach, "well, we won't have to give you any other present for your birthday!"

Dinah shook her head before enquiring, rather coolly, "So do I take it the baby was planned? It wasn't just a happy mistake?"

"Mum, you know Rupert doesn't make mistakes. He plans *everything* . . ."

Looking away from her daughter, Dinah muttered under her breath, "I have the awful feeling he worked it out, right down to the exact time required and . . ." She giggled to herself, realising it was pretty crude to say such a thing but she did wonder what bonus payment he had awarded himself for reaching his target.

Before Dinah could let her speculations run on, Johnny came in looking rather guilty. "You in some sort of trouble, Johnny?"

"No really, Mammy. It's just . . . well . . . know how I've been writing to that German lassie I met while I was doing my National Service?"

Dinah put up her hand. "We've been here before, Johnny. I know the war's been over for seven years now but your Granny Mary . . . och, Johnny, you know she's never got over Dod being killed . . ."

Johnny interrupted her. "But Granny's getting old and if Frieda was staying here she wouldn't ever need to meet her."

Sipping from a glass of water she'd just drawn from the tap, Tess gulped. "Stay *here*? Are you mad, Johnny? Our Dad never talks about what he suffered at the hands of the Germans while he was a prisoner but he did suffer. We know he did. And simply to be civil to a German would be hard enough, but to have one under his very own roof!"

"Mammy, I've invited her because I want to marry her . . ."

"Marry her?" exploded Dinah. "Oh my Gawd," she exclaimed, running her hand through her hair. "Tell me, Tess. Am I going crazy or something?"

"No, Mammy, you aren't, but our Johnny is. Look, Johnny, just leave the lassie in Germany just now. In another five years or so attitudes might – well they just might have changed."

"Cannae do that. She's arriving at the Waverley at ten

o'clock!" Johnny now turned to Tess. "She's always wanted to spend Hogmanay in Edinburgh." Turning back to Dinah he pleaded, "Mammy! Please say she can stay in the back room."

"Suppose she could, but thankfully your Uncle Archie's in residence there and there's just no way your father will put him out of that bed tonight so that a Fraulein can get in."

The long silence that now filled the room allowed Dinah's thoughts to run riot until they were suddenly interrupted, this time by Crystal bursting in. "Have you heard? Heard the awful news?" was all a tearful Crystal could sob out.

"What dreadful news is that?" Dinah asked wearily.

"Just that Sam Campbell is being sent to the Korean front line after the New Year!"

Sitting down and tugging at her hair again, Dinah wondered why Crystal's puppy-love for Sam Campbell hadn't died – but then, hadn't her Crystal's infatuation with Sam been so ardent that it had left her barking mad!

The doorbell ringing at two in the morning awoke the whole household. Joe was first to arrive at the outside door but was unable to reach the top lock. Tam arrived just as Joe was dragging a chair over to stand on. "Look, son," Tam said, as another urgent peal of the bell rang through the house, "you get back to bed and let me deal with this." Opening the door, Tam was surprised to find Patsy and Mary, both of whom seemed in quite a state. "What's the panic?" he asked.

"Panic?" screeched Mary, pushing roughly past him. "I arrive home from our Mystery Drive to Carlisle . . ."

Having now appeared on the scene, Dinah remarked,

"But I thought your Mystery Tours always went to North Berwick."

"In the summer they do. But in December we go somewhere we can do our Christmas shopping. But forget that! What's much more important is, where's my Archie? And why is there a lassie sleeping in his bed who can only say, 'Nine, nine,' when you ask her anything?"

Dinah shook her head and looked to Tam for help. "Told you, didn't I, that you should've got on to that Dag Hammarskjöld and offered him the chance to get in some experience." She turned to her mother-in-law. "That's him that's hoping to be the next United Nations Peace Keeper!"

Everybody looked from one to the other before Tam broke the silence. "Mam, Archie's in bed here. He had to get three teeth out and he didn't cope well with the anaesthetic so we decided he was better kept here with us."

Butting in, Dinah explained to Mary: "As to Frieda being in your house – she should have really been at my mother's." Dinah now looked accusingly at Patsy. "But you changed your door lock last week and forgot to give me a duplicate key so I couldn't get in. What else could I do? Frieda couldn't stay here," she went on hesitantly, "seeing she's German and Tam here isn't . . ." she paused again, searching for the right words, ". . . isn't all that well-disposed to them yet."

"Oh look, don't blame me for this fiasco. It makes no difference to me now, Dinah. The war was a long time ago. Anybody's welcome in my home now," Tam declared.

"So Frieda can come and stay in this house?"

"Aye, she's welcome . . . even if she is," he gulped, "a Teutonic kraut!"

"Did you hear that, Johnny? Your Dad says Frieda can

stay here from tomorrow and if you want to marry her you can."

"Here, just a minute," protested Tom, but as he looked around all the expectant faces in the room he knew he'd lost the argument. And as for Frieda, she'd have quite a battle on her hands getting Tam really to accept her!

22

Tom, as he was now called by everybody (with the exception of his mother and brother Archie, to whom he would always be Tam) was thoughtful as he sat in his swivel chair looking out into the snow-covered garden. New Year had come and gone but he hadn't really got into the spirit of looking forward to the new year and what it would bring.

"Well," he argued with himself, "there's not much going for it so far. Johnny'll be coming home from Germany tonight with his bride and they'll be starting married life in Johnny's room. Suppose if we'd stayed put in Restalrig Circus and I hadn't decided on going up in the world and buying this six-roomed house, Johnny wouldn't have got Dinah to agree to them staying until they'd saved up the deposit for a flat." Tom jingled the money in his pocket, thinking, "I for one couldn't help them out. Not with Dinah having to give up work because her cough had come back – and with a vengeance."

Tom's thoughts went back again to Johnny marrying in Germany with none of the family being there. Why he couldn't have got married here, he simply didn't know. Hadn't he tried to make the lassie feel, if not exactly welcome, at least tolerated?

"Oh, yes," he reminded himself, "not once did I say a word about Hitler and the German people starting the war – a war I've had cause to remember bitterly." He wriggled painfully in his chair, recalling the nightmares he still endured. Although less frequently now, he could still waken in the still of the night with terror seizing him as he imagined the cold steel of a bayoneted rifle thrusting into his back while the command, "Raus! Raus!" urged him to keep on running. Or he would relive those enforced marches where he could do nothing but trudge stoically onward. He sighed, thinking how everyone in the family said he was too cool and distant with Frieda. He huffed, thinking that even Joe had said to him, "Why don't you like her, Dad? Is it because she's not like us?" Tom gave another sigh and a slow smile crossed his face when he considered how hard it had been for him to accept Joe as "one of us". Now the wee lad had unconsciously wormed his way into his heart, so much so that he never noticed he was any different from his other children. All he knew was that Joe had brought brightness and colour into his life. He vividly remembered that evening eighteen months ago when he first realised what Joe meant to him. A constant ringing of the bell had him urgently open the door, where he found a dishevelled Dougie Small, Joe's best pal, who spluttered, "You've got to come quick, Mr Glass. Joe's injured. I even think he's deid!" Tom had raced out of the door, leaving it ajar, and followed Dougie up to the railway dyke where Dougie and he scrambled over the wall and down on to the railway line. The lungs of the wee lad were now searing and he had to stop and bend down to catch his breath.

Helping Dougie up again, Tom demanded, "Where's my Joe?" Dougie pointed along the line and over to the west where the boys regularly played football. Leaving Dougie to follow at his own pace, Tom sprinted towards the playing field and was relieved to find Joe sitting upright, his head up against another boy's chest.

"It wasnae my fault. Honest, Mister, it wisnae. Joe

was gonnae score and I tackled him and he went up in the air and came doon funny," protested Bill, another pal of Joe's.

Tom went over and lifted Joe into his arms. "I think my arm's broken in ten places and so's my leg," mumbled a tearful Joe. "And I ken I'm no supposed to . . . what's the word, Dad?"

"Trespass," said Tom. "But that's by the bye. Let's be getting you to hospital."

Joe started to tremble. "But will they no send for the polis who'll lock me up in a school for bad laddies?"

"Hardly," said Tom, unable to hide his smile. "But seeing that I'm going to have to carry you all the way, what's the easiest way out of this place?"

Joe's pals all pointed towards the railway track that ran level and was obviously the best way for Tom to carry his son.

Once they reached Leith Hospital Casualty Department, Tom was greeted by a young doctor whom he knew.

"Good evening, Mr Glass." Tom nodded as he laid Joe down on the examination trolley. "Whose wee lad is this? One of your pupils?" enquired the doctor.

Tom shook his head. "No. Joe here is my son."

The doctor briefly scrutinised both Tom and Joe before saying, "Really!"

Tom was incensed. Why was it people always noticed colour? He never did these days.

Tom knew by the incessant coughing that Dinah was about to join him. "Thought you were going to try and have a lie-in, love?"

The barking started again and it was some time before

Dinah could answer. "Naw. It just goes on and on. I'll need to see the quack again."

"How about we go down this afternoon?"

"Hmmm. Could do. He did get it sorted the last time but all he could ever say was, 'Give up the ciggies, Dinah, before they give you up!'"

Tom didn't comment. He'd been a smoker too until he became a prisoner of war. Then quickly he realised his captors wouldn't supply his basic needs in food and clothing, never mind handing out cigarettes. After the war, he'd decided that saving up the deposit for this elegant house (as he saw it) was more important than wasting money on a quick draw, so he'd never taken up the habit again. As for Dinah, he did try last year to get her to give up and she did indeed manage, accompanied by her fellow-addict, Etta. However, their success had been short-lived. The pair of them, along with Archie, went to the Palace Picture Houses to see Vincent Price in *The House of Wax*. While watching the lassie being toppled into the hot, bubbling, molten wax, Archie became so frightened that he dropped his packet of five Woodbines. Dinah and Etta then scrambled to pick them up and Archie naturally insisted they each have one. They'd readily agreed because Vincent's Wax House was so scary it was possibly going to put them all off their sleep. So surely it was better to have a puff to calm their nerves!

Before Tom and Dinah could set off for the doctor's, the doorbell rang with a characteristic clamour which indicated that Tess had arrived with her baby: the baby that was now only six months old because she'd had decided to show her father that *she* was now in charge by arriving three weeks late.

"Can't stand people who don't deliver on the date they

agreed," Rupert had announced when she was one week late – and by the time she was three weeks late he had accused the doctors of getting their calculations wrong. He'd even gone to the length of interviewing the consultant obstetrician and demanding that he be furnished with the formula that was used when the estimated time of birth was arrived at! While this request was being courteously rejected, Tess had gone into labour and Davina arrived. Of course she was called after Dinah but *never* was Davina's name to be shortened to Dinah. And small as she was, she was the one person who could make Rupert forget all his calculations and figures as he was too busy jumping through the hoops.

The instant Dinah relieved Tess of the baby, Davina began to bill and coo to her grandmother. "My, but she sure is getting on. Just look at those big blue eyes – and that smile could melt the iceberg that sunk the Titanic, so it could."

"Talking of melting, Mum, d'you know who I've just seen walking arm-in-arm along the front of the Links?"

Dinah shook her head and Tom looked nonplussed.

"Crystal and Bing!"

"Great," exclaimed Dinah. "Now if we could just get her up the aisle before wonder-boy Sam gets back from Korea . . ." Dinah couldn't go on as she was overtaken by a further bout of coughing.

"Look, Tess, just before you came in, I'd got your Mammy to agree to go to the doctor's – d'you mind if we nip out and do that? We won't be long."

"Not be long?" spluttered Dinah. "We'll be gone at least an hour. Why they don't have appointments I simply don't know." She stopped to draw in some air. "You mark my words! People will get fed up just going into a waiting room and counting the numbers in front of them." She coughed again. "You know, last week your Granny Mary was there for three hours because she kept losing count until she was the only one left in the waiting room! Now where was I? Oh aye, you mark my words – appointments will come." To please her, both Tess and Tom nodded in agreement. "Anyway, instead of you staying here, let's take wee Davina here down to see Dr Hannah. He'll be tickled pink to see her."

Once Dr Hannah had admired Davina and everybody else had left his surgery, he was then able to examine Dinah. He sighed as he removed his stethoscope from his ears and laid it on his desk. "Don't like the sound of your lungs." He paused. "Look, you go up to Spittal Street – you know, just behind the Castle – and get an X-ray done. In the meantime, I'll talk to a colleague of mine at the Eastern General Thoracic Unit and get him to see you." He paused again. "No need to ask you if you're back smoking again. I can smell it."

Dinah bowed her head in embarrassment. "I suppose I let you down."

"Not me. Yourself. Nicotine is a killer, Dinah. And you have just so much to live for!"

23

Until last week, Dinah had moaned at the length of time it took for the powers that be in the Eastern General to send her an appointment to meet the god-like figure, better known as the consultant. Dr Hannah had, after all, continually stressed to them that, in his opinion, she should be seen as a matter of urgency. Now here she was on her way at last, only a few days after the first of April, her favourite time for giving birth. Instinctively, she put her hand up and grabbed the hedge to steady herself as a bout of coughing racked her.

Then she breathed in deeply and was continuing to make her way slowly up Restalrig Road when she heard a voice call out her name from across the road. It was her mother-in-law, Mary Glass, who had obviously been waiting for her to pass that way so that she could open the window and let the whole neighbourhood know from her shouts that Dinah was going off to the hospital and so needed all the luck Mary could wish her. Waving back to let Mary know she'd heard, Dinah walked on towards the YMCA where she saw her mother already waiting for her.

Dinah had tried hard to persuade her not to come, but as Patsy herself explained, in her usual clumsy manner, she had given birth to her and if anyone was about to tell her that Dinah was going to make an early exit she would definitely be there to tell them otherwise!

They decided it would be best to enter the hospital by the back door, so they journeyed along Restalrig Crescent, crossed over Findlay Avenue and walked on to the posh side of the Crescent, which had Gumley Davidson tin hut houses on one side of the street and smart four-in-a-block corporation housing on the other.

Patsy remarked, "You know, they say folk are just desperate to get one of these tin huts. Wouldn't thank you for one, I wouldn't."

"Don't know anybody in they huts. And even if they are running with condensation, boiling in the summer and freezing in the winter, the folk inside all seem to be well-heeled."

"Aye, but they're snobs. I mean to say, just look how well you and Tom have done and you don't send your children to fee-paying schools."

Dinah was getting breathless by now and was grateful that they'd reached Findlay Gardens and the cul-de-sac that led into the allotments from where the hospital back door could be seen. "Have you ever thought, Mammy . . . that we don't send our bairns . . . to posh schools because we cannae afford it?"

"Look, you're fair puffing. Come on now. Haud on to me. I'll do the talking for once and you just listen."

By now they were in the narrow pathway that bordered the very tall hospital wall. Dinah fell against it and started to laugh uproariously. "What's so funny?" demanded Patsy, who began to rub Dinah's back after the fit of laughing had set off the coughing again.

"Nothing really," giggled Dinah, who just couldn't bring herself to explain to her mother that all her life she'd kept quiet to allow Patsy to hold court freely.

Once through the small wooden green door that took them to the rear of the hospital, Patsy said, "We'll be able to get into the thoracic unit if we go round to the left. No need to go down to the front door. That place gives me the creeps, so it does."

"Why?"

"Because," replied Patsy, indicating the hospital front with a sweep of her hand, "it's carved into the stones above the portal there that this place was opened up as the Leith Poorhouse!" She now looked all around to make sure she was not overheard – though even if she was it wouldn't matter. "And," she went on in a whisper, "they do say that Rachel Campbell – you know, Sam Campbell's mother that's a wee bit uppity . . ."

"I admire her. She's somebody to look up to," interjected Dinah.

"Oh aye, she's done a great job bringing up five bairns on her own. But they say her own mother died here of consumption when it was a Poorhouse. Then her drunken man had her dumped in a pauper's grave over there." And Patsy jabbed her thumb towards Seafield Cemetery.

When the X-rays had all been done for a second time and Dinah was now to be examined by a doctor, Patsy was much put out at not being allowed to follow her into the inner sanctum. For her part, Dinah had been grateful to have some rest from her mother's incessant babbling, though she realised that the prattling was due to Patsy having become a "nervous wreck" (as she put it) ever since Doctor Hannah had said he thought Dinah had a complaint that needed urgent attention. Dinah well understood her mother's reaction: after all, when Tess was three weeks late in giving birth to Davina, hadn't she offered to have the baby for her! But even with this insight into how a mother reacts when one of her brood is poorly, Dinah was still finding it hard to cope with her own mother.

The clock on the wall seemed to take five minutes to move on by one minute, and Patsy was on the verge of knocking at the door and asking if there was a problem, when the door opened and a nurse ushered an ashen-faced Dinah out, saying, "You will receive your appointment in the post, Mrs Glass," before she brusquely closed the door.

Immediately, Dinah put up her hand to warn her mother that this wasn't the time to ask any questions. Patsy was at a loss what to do and unconsciously she found herself saying, "I think the WVS run a wee tea shop here – d'you fancy going for a cuppa?" Dinah nodded and they made their way down to the small tea station where a well-to-do lady was in command of a tea urn and a bag of digestive biscuits. "You sit there, Dinah," Patsy suggested as she pointed to one of the three small tables in what could only be described as an oversized cupboard. "I'll get the tea. Oh look, here's your mother-in law coming. I'll just get her a cup too."

Dinah agreed as Mary looked about her sheepishly. "I ken I shouldn't hae come. But you've been that long. I was so worried. I thought," she now turned to Patsy who was returning with the tea and three digestive biscuits on a tray, "the two of you might need some . . . well, ye ken, some . . ."

A warning glance from Patsy made Mary realise that she should just sit down, drink her tea and discuss the price of bread.

24

The whole family were trying hard to keep upbeat. They nevertheless realised that the removal of a malignant tumour along with half of Dinah's left lung and some ribs, which (it was thought) would give the remaining half-lung room to breathe, was a very worrying prospect. For Dinah's part, the worst was the radiotherapy. It was so debilitating that she wished Marie Curie hadn't bothered to discover it. To be truthful, it wasn't just the continual radium sickness that was the worst. No, it was the way it had ravished her good looks. Looks that had always been so important to her.

"That you off on seven weeks' holiday, Tom?" Patsy asked, when he came into the back living room where Dinah was propped up in a chair looking out of the window.

"Think it'll be you who'll be having the holiday. And with all you've . . ."

"And Frieda," interjected Patsy, in the hope Tom would give some recognition to all the hard work Frieda had put in.

But a couple of contemptuous snorts from Tom indicated he certainly wouldn't. In his eyes Patsy deserved all the credit. "I was saying," he went on, "that with all you've done these last few weeks, keeping the home fires burning, you sure deserve a holiday." Tom toasted Patsy with a cordial wave before going over and pressing Dinah's shoulder.

Tom had underestimated Patsy. Wild horses wouldn't be able to drag her away on holiday as long as Dinah remained as poorly as she now was. She now acknowledged that Dinah had lung cancer – and also accepted Tom's assurance, based on what Dr Hannah had told him, as Dinah's next of kin, that with the removal of the tumour along with half her lung Dinah would make a full, though very slow recovery. Patsy wanted to believe Tom. She *had* to believe him. But as the weeks went by and there was no sign of any real recovery, she was beginning to have nagging doubts. And if she weren't knocking her pan in, doing so much cleaning, cooking and shopping, she would have too much time on her hands to let her fertile imagination run riot.

Further discussion as to who would be going on holiday was halted when Mary came in with an armful of newly ironed bedding which she immediately handed over to Patsy. "Good drying wind. Took them to that new launderette. Just over the way there. Remember? It used to be an ice cream shop but what a blessing the change is. You just pop your washing in as many machines as you need. Then all you have to do is put your feet up and either just watch it all going round and round till you're dizzy or else you get out your *Woman's Weekly* and, before you know it, the washing's done. Then into the dryer it gets bunged and finally a wee blaw in the back green when you get back home. And wasn't I lucky there was a nice wee wind the day. So there you are, Patsy. Got the ironing done, too, listening to *Mrs Dale's Diary*," Mary cackled. "She's worried about Jim again."

Everyone laughed. But no one made her feel that her banter was inane or pointless. She was doing all she could to help but, unlike Patsy, she feared the worst. But then Tom, her Tom, had got a wee bit fu' the night before Dinah got out of hospital and on leaving the Learig pub, he hadn't gone straight home but had made his way up to the only person he could always rely on, his own mum. She'd only opened the door to him when he immediately broke down. "Oh Mammy," he had sobbed, holding her tight. "You've just got to help me. Help me. Help all of us to be brave." Once they were through in the living room, Mary had reached down for the poker to stir the embers of the dying fire before calmly asking, "For how long?" Because of his uncontrolled sobbing, Tom's reply had been almost inaudible but she thought she had heard him splutter, "If we're lucky just . . . one . . . oh, Mammy . . . just twelve miserable months!"

"Oh, here," Mary continued, turning to Dinah. "I saw Tess and the bairn going into the shops. She'll be here in . . ."

Mary didn't need to finish as the door opened and in walked Tess. Instead of handing Davina straight over to her mother she placed her on the floor. Tess went over and stood by her mother's makeshift bed on the settee. Then she held out her arms to Davina, saying, "Come on now. You can do it."

Without any further bidding Davina staggered across the floor and flung herself into her mother's arms. "Whenever did she start walking?" Dinah crooned.

"Remember last week when Frieda and Johnny were trying to make her take a few steps?" They all nodded. "Well, when she got home she took four faltering steps and then got such a fright that she just flopped down. But would you credit it? She just wouldn't walk for her Dad. But he believed me and reckoned she would be taking twenty steps by today." Tam and Dinah exchanged a knowing look before gazing up at the ceiling. Unaware of their reaction, Tess continued, "And you know, my clever husband was absolutely right!"

For the next five minutes little Davina was treated rather like a performing seal, being bribed into walking to Patsy for a square of chocolate, to Mary for a biscuit, and finally to Tom for an orange drink.

"You know, I do like it when the family gets together," Dinah said, glancing all around the room. She had just uttered the words when Crystal and Joe came in.

Joe immediately blurted out, "Dad, have you told Mum the secret yet?"

"Joe! I'm just in the door."

"But, Dad, it's at the front door. Crystal and I saw it. And Dad," he added breathlessly, "Crystal's bet me that Mum won't believe it's yours."

"Believe what's yours?"

Tom took up a position in the middle of the floor and, looking staright at Dinah, he announced, "I've bought a car."

"A what?" gasped Dinah, and began patting her chest. "But you can't drive . . ."

"I *can* drive. Passed my test last week."

"Now, just a minute. Am I having a nightmare?"

Tom went over to the settee and took hold of Dinah's hand. "I've not been truthful with you of late."

"That so?" replied Dinah, pulling her hand away from Tom's.

"No. You see, when I told you I was taking night classes on two nights to get a bit of spare cash when I was finished at Norton Park School, Andy . . ."

"Now, how should I have not guessed that Mr Chips would have something to do with all this?"

181

Tom ignored his wife's remark and went on. "Andy gave me driving lessons in his car. He told me I was quick on the uptake, so I passed my test first time last week."

"Okay," Dinah said curtly, "but that doesn't explain the car . . ."

"A Ford Popular it is at that," chuckled Tom.

"A car!" Dinah continued. "An American car that there's a three-year waiting list for?"

"Only two years, now that they've started to manufacture them down at Doncaster."

"A car that costs about three hundred and fifty pounds?"

"Ah. But our car is five years old. Belonged to a friend of Andy's, it did, but he was buried last week so he's got no further use of it."

"But what about his family? Don't they want it?" asked Patsy.

"No. There's only his wife and she doesn't drive. However, she was adamant that it had to go to a good home – you know, to someone who would be good to it and not abuse it."

"So that's the sob-story. But how much siller did you have to cross the grieving widow's palm with before she let it go?"

Tom took a deep breath before whispering, "A hundred and fifty quid!"

"What?" exploded Dinah, sitting bolt upright on the settee and then bringing her legs around to allow them to rest on the floor. "Are you telling me that we're now up to our eyeballs in debt to the tune of one hundred and fifty quid? Some bloody grieving widow!"

"We're *not* in debt. I'd already saved up fifty pounds – which included Crystal pitching in her ten bob overtime every week for the last three months. But when Andy's pal died quicker than we thought he would, Andy, the good pal that he is, offered to give me a no-interest loan for the hundred pounds I was short. I'll pay him back at a pound a week. And that's only ten bob each from Crystal and me."

No one said a word. They all knew Dinah was seething. Tom always did what Andy thought he should be doing and they agreed with Dinah when she demanded, "But why does Andy want to help you like this?"

"No me. You!"

"Me?"

"Aye. You see, when I told him how much you were missing getting out and about, he thought that if I could first learn to drive and then get my licence he would lend me his car to take you anywhere you wanted to go. He said that under the circumstances you wouldn't want him to be chauffeuring you."

Dinah's was not the only head to bow in embarrassment. Mary, her mother-in-law, had also thought there was something not quite right about the relationship between Andy and her Tam, so she too felt more than a little sheepish.

Tom had tried to explain it to them, but they just didn't understand, that during those five long years in captivity, when they had always had to look out for one other, to share with each other – or die – a bond had grown up between the two men. And it would always exist. Especially for Andy, who had never married because the lassie he would have married had been killed on active service in France.

"So the car is to take me out for wee trips, is it? How many does it seat?"

"Officially – four. But we'll be able to squeeze in six if

two are bairns." He now looked at Patsy and Mary, who he could see were wondering whether they were to be included in these trips and so he added, "Or *like* bairns!"

Dinah was now smiling. She rose and slipped her arm through Tom's. "Suppose we'd better have a look at this limousine before I wake up and I find it's all been a dream."

The whole family piled out into the street. Proudly, Tom took up residence in the driver's seat, with Dinah in the front passenger seat. All the others, not to be outdone, took it in turns to sit in the back. Patsy was delighted to shout over to Tom: "That's me, your Mammy, Myra and Joe all in, and we're quite comfortable."

Dinah chuckled, "They're no able to breathe but they're quite comfortable. Just as well Elsie's out with her pal – or should I say a lumber?"

"So you like it?"

"Aye. Where'll we go to first? I've only been back and forth to the blooming hospitals these past few months."

"How about after tea we go on a Mystery Tour?" suggested Mary.

"Aye, let's go to North Berwick and I'll pay for the fish and chips when we stop at Port Seton!" crooned Patsy.

Tom and Dinah exchanged an amused look. Of course! Where else would a Mystery Tour take you to but North Berwick?

When the car set off on its inaugural mystery drive, Joe was sitting on Mary's knees, as she didn't sport the ample stomach of Patsy, who had Myra on her lap. This arrangement had come about because Dinah thought that, since Crystal had stumped up for the car, so that her mother could be taken out, she'd every right to be included in the first trip. Accordingly, Crystal was now securely crushed between her two grandmothers.

While the others were all busily getting ready for the jaunt, Dinah had time to talk to Crystal. "Thought you might have had other things to be saving for – forbye the car," said Dinah, patting the space beside her on the couch.

Shaking her head, Crystal obediently sat down beside her mother. "Not really."

"Thought you and Bing might be . . . you know."

"He'd like us to get engaged . . . och, but I'm not sure. He's nice and he's comfortable to be with but . . ."

"You still carrying a torch for Sam Campbell?"

Crystal's face fired. "No. I don't really care that he's coming home in September."

"No," Dinah thought to herself, "but you cared enough to find out when he was due home. She looked at Crystal, the plainest of all her children and yet the one you could always depend on, and she wished her daughter would stop longing for a Prince Charming – who, to be truthful, very rarely ended up with Cinderella!

The run to East Lothian proved a great success. Everyone on board was more excited than a child on its birthday. North Berwick was so very beautiful. Tom and Dinah had sat on a bench and looked out over the picturesque sea, marvelling at the mystical Bass Rock that sat serenely a few miles off-shore. "How many artists do you think have painted this scene?" Tom asked Dinah.

Dinah just shrugged her shoulders. She didn't really care. What mattered to her was that she was out in the wide world again. That she was free. That she could see once more the wild and romantic sea that had always mesmerised her. That she would get safely back home. Right back home to their own front door – and all courtesy of the car.

All too soon it was time to head for home – to pile into the vehicle again and make for the little fishing village of Port Seton where newly landed fish would be expertly fried in batter and served up to them with golden crunchy chips. The scrumptious feast would then be washed down with Red Cola.

Having left Port Seton, Tom thought he would give them a treat and take them for a run around East Lothian. Somehow, because Tom really didn't know the district, they landed up in Haddington. On leaving Haddington, they headed towards Tranent and had just left there when Tom realised that he would have to tackle a winding downward road that was unfamiliar to him. At the bottom of an incline, the car suddenly shuddered. The engine stuttered. Then the car ground slowly to a halt.

"Oh, blast!" was the cry from Tom. "Now, Andy did say that it sometimes does this. Don't panic. No need to worry. Right, Crystal. You and Granny Patsy get out and start pushing from the back and I'll get out and push, with the door open, from the front. When the car engine roars into life again – and it will – you must run as fast as you can and jump in."

"Jump into a moving car? Who do you think I am? Yon flying Dutch woman, Fanny what's her name?" moaned Patsy.

"Look, it'll be quite all right, Patsy. You just make sure you push from the back on the left-hand side. Because that'll mean you'll be jumping back into the car ahead of . . ."

"Mugsy! And what'll happen to me if I don't get round fast enough or Granny's ample rear-end blocks the door?" demanded Crystal.

"The two of you have to be really quick. Because once I've got the car running again I can't stop. Here," Tom now pulled a sixpence from his pocket and handed it to Crystal, "If anything goes wrong – but it won't – you can catch a bus home at Levenhall."

"Levenhall! But that's miles away."

"Will you all stop whining? You're upsetting your mother and the most important thing is that we get her home in time for her medication."

Patsy and Crystal took up their stations behind the car. Joe, who was in charge of keeping the back door open for Patsy and Crystal to jump in, was much more interested in what his father was busy doing and therefore was holding the door only half open.

Tom shouted the command for Patsy and Crystal to start pushing, while he steered, shoved and sprinted forward. Of course, Tom had no experience of the roads in East Lothian and was quite unaware that the road out of Tranent was steep and winding. Quite suddenly, he panicked as the car went round a bend. Before he could straighten it up, he was faced with another bend – then another – and yet another. Each time they turned a corner, the car went faster and faster. It had now gained such momentum that he could hardly keep up. Reluctantly he decided the best solution was for him to jump back in and yank the brakes on. Just as he was about to leap in, the engine roared into life. "Run for it now," he shouted as he leapt aboard and slammed his door shut as the car raced away.

Unfortunately, it was all too much for Patsy and when

Tom shouted, "Run for it," she stopped to get her breath back. A belated attempt to jump led to her falling face-down in the road with Crystal landing on top of her. All they could then do was wail in anguish as the car disappeared from view round the next bend.

The pair of them had been sitting there for no more than a couple of minutes when they heard the clip-clop of hooves and along came a horse and cart. "You could easy get yourself killed sitting there," warned the farmer who was driving. "It's hay-time, you know."

Crystal nodded. "Our car broke down and when it got going again it went off without us."

The farmer looked bewildered. "Drove off on its own, did it?"

"No, my Dad was driving but he's just learned and once he got the car going again he was too frightened to stop."

"So he left you and your mother to get on with it?"

"She's not my mother. She's my Granny. Look. Could you please give us a lift to a bus stop?"

"That's no problem."

"Thank you."

"But, Miss, the real problem is that there won't be a bus until tomorrow morning!"

"You're joking!"

"No. Now, if you could get yourselves to Musselburgh – though that's a long, long walk – you could get a bus there."

Crystal started to realise that she would have to get on this man's good side, so she wheedled, "Look, Mister, my Granny's *very old* and she has the rheumatics. Could you maybe let us sit up on your hay bales and take us to Musselburgh?"

"Suppose I could," drawled the man. "Especially if you was to make it worth my while."

Crystal held out her sixpence. The man shook his head and chewed on a piece of tobacco before proposing, "But if you, the young one, were to promise to come back this weekend and help me and the missus on the farm, I could . . ."

Crystal didn't wait for him to finish. "Done!" she shouted as she began to hoist Patsy on to the cart and then jumped up herself.

25

All the women seated round the table smiled with relief when the power was switched off and the noise in the bottling plant ceased. Break times were always so welcome in the Bond. Times when you could have a ten-minute break. And what was even more appreciated was the thirst-quenching cup of tea from the tea trolley.

They'd all collected their tea from the trolley and were now back chatting when Ina Stewart, her mouth full of biscuits, said, "Here, Crystal, think I've won my bet?"

"Not quite," Crystal replied. "You see, I'm not exactly going *down* to the Halloween Dance with Sam Campbell . . ."

"See. I bet you a couple of bob that lover-boy would never go with you. So stump it up."

"No. You see, he's going to meet up with Chalky and his cousin first – so he asked me to go to the Assembly Rooms with his sisters – you know, Carrie and Alice."

"So that means I've won my bet."

"No," argued Crystal. "You see, he's meeting me at the dance hall."

Crystal's response was met with half the group sniggering and nudging each other, and the other half (mainly the older women) just nodding their heads wisely and regretting Crystal having been given a dizzie, as they put it.

At two o'clock in the morning, the house in Restalrig Road was so quiet that even the scampering of a field-mouse out in the garden would have sounded like a herd of stampeding elephants. So Crystal, shoes in hand, opened the outside door very quietly and then crept in. But Dinah was awake. "That you, Crystal?" she called out in a loud whisper.

Opening the door to the back lounge, where her mother now slept, Crystal entered and crossed to the settee. "Sorry, Mammy. I didn't want to waken you."

"I was awake anyhow," answered Dinah. "Did you have a good time? Please tell me that it was Betty Grable, the girl with the million-dollar legs, who won."

Crystal let out a long, weary sigh. "I'd no chance. But worse still. Oh, Mammy, you were right. I should never have gone chasing after Sam Campbell."

"What happened?" Dinah asked earnestly, moving over on the couch so that there was room for Crystal to sit down.

"It's a long story," replied Crystal, settling down beside her mother. Crystal enjoyed the intimacy because it reminded her of when she was a wee girl and either Granny Patsy or her mother would sort out any problems she had.

"And I've got all night," said Dinah. That remark confirmed for Crystal that perhaps her mother would know how to deal with her dilemma.

"Well, Mammy, everything was going well. The pubs had closed and we were all there. I was dancing with Sam and we were getting on great, when this Rita Hayworth look-alike arrived. Honestly, Mammy, you should have seen her. There wasn't a man in the hall that wasn't drooling. And who was the lucky devil she got in tow with – none other than Sam Campbell! Anyway, she won the fancy-dress competition hands down and Sam was going to walk her home." Crystal huffed and puffed before going on. "We'd all started to walk over the Links without Sam when Chalky ran back and punched Rita a shot." Crystal started to laugh and she leant back against her mother before continuing, "Sorry to be laughing but the more I think of it! Rita went head over heels and her wig fell off but that wasn't the worst of it. Her big bosom burst and squealed itself flat – because, oh, Mammy, they were only balloons and when we all looked at her, bald and deflated, we realised that Rita was a Roger!"

"You mean he was a transvestite?"

"Oh, I don't know what religion he is. I only know he was a man dressed as a woman and Sam Campbell – ha ha – she made him look the right idiot he is."

"So you now realise he's not for you?"

Rising and going into the kitchen to put the kettle on, Crystal said, "Aye. I know now that all these years I've been hoping . . . well, hoping that he'd see that I'd grown up and wasn't any longer a silly gawky lassie, but . . ." She gave out a little snigger and sniffed philosophically before adding, "You're right, Mammy. Time to move on."

When Crystal came back into the room with two steaming cups of tea, Dinah asked, "So you've definitely decided to forget dashing Sam?" Crystal nodded. "And how do you propose to do that?"

"Think I might take a walk over to the Crematorium tomorrow. What time do they open the gates on a Saturday?"

The first of the winter frost had settled on the cemetery grounds and Crystal thought how the white dusting gave the grounds an eerie appearance.

She'd made her way halfway through from the Pirniefield entrance when a man began to run towards her waving his arms.

"Oh, hello, Bing. Fancy seeing you here."

"I work here. Isn't it you that's not in the right place?"

Crystal started to laugh. "I see what you mean. I'm just on my way to visit one of the women I work with in the Bond. She has one of those bungalows in Craigentinny Avenue North."

"One of those?" mused Bing. "I always think that houses as fine as those in that street should have been built somewhere much nicer. I mean, would *you* like to have an outlook to the rubbish dump – not to mention also having to put up with the Seafield pong? You know, that stink makes this place smell like Paris in the spring."

Crystal shook her head. "Suppose so. But, you know, some of the people there might prefer where they are to a flat in Jameson Place."

"Suppose you're right. But what would *you* prefer?"

Taking time to consider her reply, Crystal eventually said, "I suppose . . . a nice cosy flat, like you have, would be best. Handy for the shops and all."

Bing dragged the toe of his shoe over the frosty ground and kept his head lowered as he spoke: "In that case it's still on offer."

Six weeks later the whole family, with the exception of Dinah, who had so desperately wanted to be there, were all crowding into the small dingy registry office in Fire Brigade Street (officially known as Junction Place) to witness Crystal and Bing being married.

It had been quite a rush getting everything organised.

But Bing had insisted they marry as soon as possible – before Crystal changed her mind again.

For her part, Crystal would have liked a wedding where she'd have been resplendent in a long white gown with matching veil and train. She felt somewhat short-changed to be standing there in a bright pink dress and jacket that had been made for her by the seamstress at the bottom of Restalrig Road. And adding to the fact that the dress looked so obviously handmade, there was no music and no flowers. She'd often dreamed of her wedding day but somehow today just didn't match up – especially as one of her workmates came in with a laden message bag out of which a turnip, some carrots and a couple of leeks were protruding. "Judy, God bless her, was the only one in Bond Nine not to have marked the date on the calendar," thought Crystal. The Bond girls were of course not the only ones to remark when they heard of the rushed wedding, "Time alone will tell!"

"Tell what?" fumed Crystal. "Surely I'm not the only twenty-two, going on twenty-three-year-old virgin in the whole of Leith?" Crystal now thought of her workmates and she gave a devilish giggle as she thought, "Well, I could be – after all, I'm the only one who's never been inside Fairley's dance hall."

Crystal was now being asked by the registrar to take up her position beside Bing, who was looking, as usual, as if he'd put in an effort to be tidy but somehow hadn't quite made it. He was, however, fully aware of the solemnity of the occasion and was standing so stiff and upright that it seemed as if he had a brush handle stuck up his back. Even the arrival of Crystal at his side failed to make him relax. Before they knew it, they had mutually agreed to spend the rest of their natural lives together and the family were crowding around to offer their congratulations. Crystal felt deeply moved when her tearful father kissed her on both cheeks and wished her well.

The reception, if it could be called that, was to be up at Restalrig Road, where a very frail and ailing Dinah could be included in the festivities. To save work, Tom had gone to Crawford's up-market bakery in Leith's Elbe Street and ordered their best purvey. The feast of pies, sausage rolls, sandwiches, cakes and scones had been delivered on three bread boards and the first thing the guests had to do was to help set it all out as a buffet.

Once the time arrived to toast the happy couple and cut the cake – courtesy of the Home Bakery where Granny Patsy still worked – Dinah insisted on standing with a glass of sherry in her hand. Crystal looked towards her mother and a shiver ran down her spine. She had heard that with some people you could see the hand of death resting on their shoulders. Up until now, she'd felt it was an old wife's tale, but today, as she accepted everyone's good wishes, she knew her mother was living on borrowed time.

After three hours, when most of the guests, except for the family, had left in order to allow Dinah to get some rest, Tom indicated to Crystal and Bing that it was time to leave for the airport.

When the discussion had arisen earlier of where Crystal and Bing should honeymoon, Tom's friend Andy suggested that, since Crystal was not having a lavish wedding, wouldn't it be nice for her to have a honeymoon that would be the envy of most people? All agreed on that proposal and a week had been booked in a *pension* in the resort of Lloret de Mar on the Costa Brava! Bed and breakfast, together with an evening meal, were all supplied but at a costly thirty pounds each – a whole month's wages, no less. This expenditure was met by Tom and the two Grannies all giving presents of money, which Granny Patsy pointed out was best – other types of presents not really being needed since Bing had his own house.

It wasn't until the holiday was actually being booked and paid for that Crystal discovered they would both need passports to be able to leave the country and to be allowed into Spain.

The problem was that the Passport Office that they would have to visit in order to get their passports urgently was in Liverpool. Immediately, Tom had offered his precious Ford Popular to Bing so that he could drive Crystal and himself all the way to Merseyside to obtain the documents needed for the fairytale honeymoon to go ahead.

As the evening flight took off from Edinburgh for Spain, Crystal, still clutching her precious passport, began to feel increasingly apprehensive. Not once during the last month had she taken the time to consider if she was doing the right thing. But now, as the plane soared heavenwards, she looked towards Bing, who was seated beside her. Did she *really* want to spend the rest of her life with him? Was her longing for Sam Campbell well and truly buried? It was Bing asking her if she was as happy as he was that made her resolve that she would do all in her power to make the marriage work and never have Bing regret the step he had just taken.

A week is a long time when someone is as desperately ill as Dinah. She'd been so poorly in the last week that she'd said to Tom, "Look, love, no need to lie any more. We all know that I'm dying." Tom took her hand in his as she shook her head. "We have to talk – there are things I want to say." It was quite true that she did have things she wanted to say but morbid fatigue quickly overtook her and she fell sound asleep.

While she slept Tom never moved from her side and when she awoke, quite unaware of having been asleep, Dinah took up from where she'd left off. "Tom, it's about Joe. I spoke to Crystal and asked whether, if ever anything was to happen to me, she would take him."

His body stiff with anger, Tom jumped to his feet. "Do you really think that if ever you weren't here, Joe wouldn't belong with me? Oh, Dinah! He's my son! Being someone's biological parent doesn't automatically make you their dad. A dad is the man who walks the floor with you when you have the mumps. A dad is the one who worries when you're out late. A dad is the one who provides for you, feeds you, clothes you ... loves you, loves you enough to forgive you anything." He paused before continuing in a faltering yet determined voice, "Even having been born from another man's seed!"

Tears were now running down Dinah's cheeks and when Tom saw them he mellowed. Wiping her eyes, he said, "I love him. Of all our children, he's the most like you. He has your brilliance – your zest for living – your continual pushing of the boundaries. Losing either of you will break my heart; but I couldn't go on living if I lost you both."

Dinah nodded and said, "The only other thing I want to say is this. I know I'm Catholic, and my mother will want me buried in Mount Vernon Cemetery, but I would like this *thing* that's killing me – taking me away from all of you, all you folk that I love – I want to have it cremated. Burnt to a cinder and then my ashes thrown to the wind down on Portobello beach!"

"Is that all you want?" enquired a solemn Tom, who was prepared to pull the moon down for her if she asked for it.

Dinah thought long and hard before she looked up into his eyes. "Remember when we were young and how we used to walk hand-in-hand from Seafield, along Portobello Prom and on to Joppa?" Tom nodded. "Any chance we could go there again? I'd like to see the shore, watch the crashing waves and see the pictures in the clouds as they hurry by." Tom didn't answer. It didn't seem much but in her condition it was obviously impossible. Dinah plucked at the blanket that covered her. "You know, Tom, I know it's a lot to ask but I know who would help us do it."

"You do?" was all Tom could mumble.

"Aye. Andy! Yes, why don't you ask dear old Mister Chips?"

Dinah always told her children that they should walk along the sunlit shore in Portobello during December if they wanted to be exhilarated and captivated by its beauty. But only if you were lucky enough to be an artist could you capture the moment.

"Try," she would urge them, "to go when the tide has ebbed and the deep crimson rays of the morning sun lights up the millpond-like sea – making it appear blood-red. Or else go when the tide is so energetic that as it crashes against the sea wall it flies upwards in a foaming torrent – a foaming torrent of spray that quickly bursts and is dragged back protesting over the musical shale. Look up at the clouds, children, as I have done so often, and watch them changing shape as they chase one another over the heavens. See them scurry to help the wind whip the sea into a frenzy which makes it seem like a maelstrom dragging all it can back into its own domain."

Dinah vividly remembered what she had taught her children when she sat in the wheelchair that Andy had borrowed. She patiently waited for Tom to tuck a blanket over her knees. Then he would push her all the way along to Joppa where Andy would be ready to help get her into the car again and bring her safely home.

As they moved off, Dinah felt her prayers had actually been answered. The December day was cold but bright. The white-crested waves were visible far out to sea and when they came to crash noisily on the shore their strength and magnificence overwhelmed her. How she longed to regain just a few bursts of their undying energy. With that, she would dance along the sand in her bare feet, as she had so often done as a girl. She remembered fondly how she'd often turned round to find Tom chasing her. Tom, who would never even take off his socks and allow the water to run between his toes as he paddled in the sea.

All too soon they were past the open-air swimming pool and she shuddered to recall how often she'd swum there in the freezing July water. How she'd paraded bravely in her bikini, with her skin turning blue because she wouldn't wrap up. On they went together, past the amusement park, and were approaching the indoor swimming pool at the foot of Bellfield Street when Tom pushed the chair towards a bench. He swung her round to face the turbulent sea and sat down. "Happy?" he asked. "Is this what you wanted?"

Holding back her tears, Dinah nodded before saying, "Don't tell me you don't remember."

Unlike Dinah, he was unable to hide his grief and all he

could mutter was, "You know, when I was taken prisoner, at night when we were cold and hungry, I used to think about the two of us on Portobello Prom. I know you won't believe this – but sometimes just picturing the cold rushing tide in my mind warmed me up. Heated me so well that the desolation was made bearable." He faltered and his voice cracked before he could go on. "You see, I knew that one day I would get back to you! My determination to return to you saved my life."

Dinah leant sideways and took his hand in hers. They looked lovingly at one another but nothing more was said. There was no need for any more words.

Crystal had arrived home on the evening flight and, no matter how much she wanted to see her mother again, it was just too late to disturb the household.

So it wasn't surprising that as soon as Bing left for work the next morning, she quickly tidied up before dashing to Stories the bakers in Leith Walk. "Eight rolls and a round of well-fired bran scones," she hurriedly requested from the dilatory shop assistant. "And could you please be quick? I want to catch the next bus to Restalrig."

The house door was never locked these days, to allow the family, doctors and friends to come in quietly, and so Crystal was in the back living room before anyone knew she was there.

The room, Crystal knew, would be thoroughly cleaned daily. Yet, no matter how much Dettol they used or how hard her two Grannies and Frieda worked, they were unable by now to mask the odour of Dinah's mortal decay. The stench frightened Crystal and when it invaded her nostrils she had to suppress the urge to throw up. Another feature that disturbed her was the ghostly half-light in the sickroom. Before going to draw back the curtains and let in the limited December daylight, she checked to see whether the large easy chair that her father now slept in was vacant. A sigh of relief escaped her when she discovered that it was indeed empty. But, before she could let the light in, a voice behind her whispered, "Thought you were a figment of my imagination."

Crystal turned and gladly let her father's arms encircle her. "No. I got home last night. Wanted to come and see you then but Bing said it was just too late. Anyway, I knew you'd all be settled down for the night."

"Is that really you, Crystal?" Dinah's weakened voice called out.

Releasing herself from her father, Crystal went over to her mother. "Yeah, Mam, it's me. And just wait till I tell you all about my adventure."

Dinah struggled to pull herself up on the couch. "Good. But could you do it while you give me a quick wee dicht?"

"Of course. But you must promise to save me from Granny Patsy's wrath when she finds out I've taken over her duties." Dinah nodded and they both giggled.

Tom interrupted them. "When you came in, Crystal, I was just about to go and rouse Elsie for her work and then get Joe and Myra ready for school, so I'll go and get on with those things now." He ran his hand over the stubble on his chin and added, "But I think I'll take up residence in the bathroom first."

As soon as her father had left, Crystal set about making Dinah more comfortable. As she washed her mother's sunken cheeks and massaged her bony hands, she babbled on about Lloret de Mar. It was no more than idle banter that stopped her showing Dinah how shocked she was at seeing the deterioration the last week had brought. Here was her mother, the most beautiful of creatures, ravaged by a disease that none of them properly understood. Crystal choked back her fear before saying in the brightest tone she could summon, "Oh, Mammy, I know how much you like the beach and the sea. I just wish I could take you to Lloret de Mar. Believe me, even in December it's warm enough to picnic on the shore. I just sat in a deck chair and watched the sea coming and going. It was all so lovely."

"Nothing is more lovely than Portobello in the winter when it's just us locals who brave the elements and simply enjoy looking at the view." A short silence followed before Dinah croaked, "Do you know what Portobello means?" Crystal shook her head. "Beautiful port. My lovely beautiful port."

Crystal thought her mother was perhaps growing over-sentimental, so quickly changed the subject by asking, "Did you miss me? Enjoy the wedding reception?"

"I did. And every day I was wondering how you were getting on."

"Oh, we were fine. Bing told me," confided Crystal, "about how his mother couldn't cope after his father was killed in the war."

"Is she still alive?" Crystal nodded silently.

"I didn't know that."

"Nobody knew. She's now in Bangour Village Hospital and you know how nobody wants to say they have a relative in an asylum. Poor Bing doesn't think she'll ever get out. Said she'd been there so long she was becoming institutionalised and wouldn't ever be able to cope in the outside world."

"Does he go to see her?"

"Yes. And I'm going to go with him. You don't need to worry about her coming out because our house was never hers. It was his granny's and when her son, Bing's dad, was killed she changed her will and left it to Bing."

It was now time for Dinah to ask the questions that she was burning to ask. "Crystal," she said, plucking nervously at her blankets, "are you happy?" Crystal nodded. "I mean, *really* happy?"

"Don't know about being *really* happy. Don't even know what that means. But I do know that I'm quite content. Bing's a good man. He's had a sad life but now I know he loves me – and he really *does* love me." She stopped, brought up her leg and playfully slapped it. "He even loves this crooked old leg of mine. That being the case, I'm determined to be a good wife to him. Keep his home. Have his kids. I'm so grateful."

Dinah fell back on her pillows again. "But," she whispered, taking Crystal's hand in hers and giving a sigh, "you haven't said if he makes you happy. Really happy. I do so want you to be happy like your Dad and I are."

"I've told you, Mammy. I'm content. He's good to me." Crystal hesitated. She thought it would be quite wrong not to answer her mother honestly. Even though her mother was dying, Dinah wouldn't want Crystal to deceive her. So Crystal continued, while stroking her mother's brow, "Oh, Mammy, if you want to know whether Bing makes me sing in the morning – then I have to say truthfully that the answer is *no*!"

26

The family had hoped that by March the numbing cold they had felt ever since Christmas Eve, when Dinah had quietly passed away in her sleep, would now have started to thaw. Relatives, friends and neighbours had all been very kind and considerate to Tom and Dinah's children. But it was going to take a lot more than endless pots of soup and rice puddings from Granny Patsy, not to mention extra bags of coal from Tom's old school pal, before there was any lessening of that paralysing chill that had engulfed them on Hogmanay, when they had said goodbye to Dinah at Seafield Crematorium.

Joe and Myra, whom everyone bent over backwards to care for, seemed to be the only ones to welcome the blizzards that had cut off northern communities this winter. Thanks to Andy, who again happened to have a friend who had died leaving a brand-new television, they could now tune into what was going on in the country and they laughed when they saw aeroplanes dropping supplies to the stranded in the north of Scotland.

When not glued to the television watching *Wagon Train*, the pair were down sledging on Leith Links. They were adamant that Leith Links, unlike the rest of Edinburgh, was not in the grip of the freezing spell and that therefore they were perfectly safe. Safe indeed they were until Myra tumbled off her sledge as it went careering down the Plague Mound and she gaped in horror when the blood from her gashed forehead sprinkled the pristine snow.

Joe, who was now eleven and well-developed for his years, should have been looking after her. However, as he was happily basking in the adoration being given him by a group of teenage females who seemed bowled over by his charm and good looks, Joe was far too busy to be looking after Myra.

When one of the boys, who all wanted to be like Joe, called out that Myra was hurt, Joe panicked. He knew his dad was apt to turn everything into a drama these days. Life would have been so much easier for them all if his dad had simply screamed that he didn't want Dinah to die and that he didn't wish to live without her. If only he'd kicked the cat and sworn at Frieda. But he did none of these things. Yet, when some little thing went wrong, it became a federal case.

Joe was struggling to drag a reluctant and sobbing Myra up the road to find someone who could tend her wound when one of the school teachers who taught in Leith Academy Primary appeared and asked if she might help. Joe felt he really didn't need her assistance but she insisted on taking Myra into her home to tend the bleeding forehead. Then she firmly instructed Joe to go and fetch his father. "And only your father, mind you!"

He had just unfolded the whole story to his father, saying that Miss Cole insisted that he should go to collect Myra, when Frieda said, "Oh no. I know Miss Cole all too well, so I think I should go and fetch Myra."

"Why?" asked Johnny.

"Because she and quite a few others would dearly like to console your father."

"So?"

"Oh, Johnny. There's consoling and there's consoling!

And, believe me, Miss Cole's idea of consoling will be candlelight suppers and counselling on the settee."

Tom was furious that Frieda thought he would be daft enough to fall for such trickery. Before anyone could stop him, Tom had fled from the house and sprinted down the road.

After an hour had gone by and neither Tom nor Myra had returned, Frieda stood up and announced she would go to Miss Cole's house to bring both of them back home.

After she had rung the bell three times, the door was reluctantly opened by Miss Cole who said, "I'm very busy. Could you come back tomorrow?"

"*Nein,*" was the curt reply as Frieda pushed past her and looked in each room in turn. Eventually she went into a small bedroom and gasped when she saw Myra, with a bandaged head, all tucked up in bed but with no sign of Tom. "Right!" she said to bewildered Myra in a most Teutonic tone. "You come with me – *mach schnell*! Now, where is your father?"

Myra willingly scrambled from the bed and raced out of the door followed by Frieda. They both had to halt abruptly at the study door since it was being fiercely guarded by Miss Cole. That lady had underestimated Frieda, who promptly stamped on her foot so hard that Miss Cole not only yelped in pain but fell so hard against the door that it flew open.

Frieda could do nothing else but laugh at the pitiful sight that she saw as she looked into the room – there stood a tie-less, jacketless, shoeless and sockless Tom trying to climb out of the window. "Tut, tut!" she said, in her most disapproving voice. "What on earth is going on here?"

By now Miss Cole had managed to compose herself. "I

was engaged in the 'laying on of hands'," she announced, trying to push Tom back on a chair. "It is a well-known method of bringing consolation to the bereaved."

"That right?" retorted Frieda, grabbing hold of Tom and thrusting his clothes into his hands. "Well, I can assure you that you are free to lay your hands on anyone you like – but get your hands off him. He's mine. And I have my own ways of making him better!"

Tam looked flabbergasted. "Look, I'm nobody's but my own. And I don't want . . ."

Frieda gave him another fierce push. "Quiet! Get yourself dressed. We go home now. Myra's wanting her cocoa. And for you, Tom, I am going to make you a nice German toddy – you know, schnapps and schnapps and more schnapps!"

Carrying Myra, Tom and Frieda made their way back up Restalrig Road without a word being said. When they arrived home Tom immediately turned to Frieda and was about to remonstrate when she put up her hand. "No need to thank me for saving you from that man-eater. But you know, Tom, you should have been in Germany during the war and you would have been more worldly wise than you are now." Tom wanted to remind Frieda that he had been a guest of the Third Reich for five years and that their cruelty was something he would never forget but Frieda went on relentlessly: "Surely you know that handsome widowers like you are always much sought after."

A peal of laughter resonated around the room. "My Dad being sought after?" chuckled Johnny.

"Oh yes! He will be. And don't you forget, Johnny Glass, I fell in love with you because you are so much like your Dad."

Tom looked at Frieda. He'd never given her a chance. He

had to admit she'd been his mainstay ever since Dinah had fallen ill. She had nursed Dinah meticulously, never allowing herself to feel disgusted when attending to Dinah's most basic needs. After Dinah's death, she'd cooked and cleaned, looked after the children and held the whole family together. It was time now, he thought, to say thank you. "Frieda," he began hesitantly, "I just want you to know how much I admire and appreciate what you've done for us all and . . . Oh blast it! I love you like a daughter, I do."

Frieda went over and kissed Tom lightly on the cheek. "Thank you, *mein Lieb*. And now you make me feel guilty, you see . . . Johnny, you must tell him."

"Dad, Frieda's pregnant." Everyone in the room clapped their hands and shouted congratulations. Johnny held up one hand. "Quiet. I haven't finished. And we've managed to get a wee house, so we'll be leaving you all to get on with it."

Tom sank down on a chair. How on earth was he going to manage without Frieda? Frieda the Kraut that he never wanted his son to marry. Frieda whom he now needed so badly. She in turn sensed his fear and said, with a wink towards Johnny, "But Tom, we're only moving further down Restalrig Road. In fact we'll be in a flat on the right-hand side of the road and that little flat looks straight into Miss Cole's house. So, my dear Tom, if ever she decides to go up the road instead of *down* – with friendly persuasion – I'll have her change direction!"

27

Tom was determined that this Christmas would be a real family Christmas like the ones they'd had before they lost Dinah. But how, he wondered, would he achieve this – because, one year on, everyone's grief was still so very raw. Frieda came up trumps, however, by giving birth to a seven-pound baby girl. The baby was officially to be called Patricia but already that was shortened, not to Patsy (after whom she was called) but to Tricia.

The new baby caught everybody's attention, especially since she and her parents were living with Tom. This arrangement had come about because Frieda missed having a back door and a garden to hang her washing in. So when a lower-flatted wreck of a villa became vacant in Pirniefield, just off Restalrig, Johnny and Frieda had put in a ridiculously low offer and were overjoyed when it was accepted.

Luckily, their own small flat in Restalrig Road sold very quickly. The Pirniefield house, however, did require quite a bit of work done before it was habitable and so, to minimise the financial outlay, the task of repairing the solid house to the standard of all those around it fell to Johnny and Tom, both of whom were expert tradesmen.

Rupert had done his usual calculations and came to the conclusion that, even if the house had been a steal, Johnny and Frieda would require some financial help. He also reckoned that, as both Tom and Johnny worked full-time and would only be able to work on the house in their spare time, it would take at least three months before the family could move in.

Rather to Rupert's surprise, Tom seemed delighted to agree with him. But Tess's husband was really put out when Tom suggested that Johnny, Frieda and his grandchild, Tricia, should move back in with him.

Tess, who was becoming more and more like her husband and was now being eaten up by jealousy, made a point of seeking out Crystal to ask what she thought of the Pirniefield mystery. Crystal replied, "Look here, Tess, the only mystery I'm interested in right now is why I've been married for a whole year and yet I'm still not expecting!"

"Oh," huffed Tess, "I thought you were just waiting till you'd saved up enough to get out of that pokey wee flat in Jameson Place."

"Jameson Place is *not* pokey. It's bright and cosy."

"Anything you say, Mrs Nippy," retorted Tess.

Crystal continued to speak – but more to herself. "And Bing and I want a family right *now*! And my brooding has got worse ever since Tricia arrived. I just love nursing her, walking her out in her pram. And . . . she's so like Mum."

"Oh, if that's all it takes to make you happy, then I've good news for you." Crystal looked expectantly over to Tess who now appeared to be seething with bitterness as she went on: "You see, I'm having another baby in June and we never meant to have another one for two years. I'm not Superwoman, so I'll need all the help I can get to cope with two bawling infants!"

This news upset Crystal. "You mean you're expecting *by accident*?"

Tess sighed. "Yes. Rupert did calculate the safe dates by the rhythm method but somehow or another . . ."

A gale of laughter from Crystal echoed round the house, bringing both Tom and Granny Patsy rushing in to discover what all the hilarity was about. Crystal pointed to Tess and exclaimed, "You lot won't believe it, but our ever-cautious Rupert got so carried away with the rhythm that he added a few beats of his own and now our Tess's jiggered!"

"Dad! Granny!" Tess protested. "She means I'm pregnant and that's no laughing matter."

Before Tom could speak, in dashed twelve-year-old Joe. "Dad! Dad, just wait till I tell you." Everyone waited with bated breath before Joe went on, "I've just been picked to play for the school's first team."

This was what Tom had long been hoping for. Joe was indeed promising to become a gifted footballer. His dad had known, as soon as Joe became a pupil at Norton Park Secondary School, that it would only be a matter of time until his prowess on the football team was recognised.

Granny Patsy, who was also convinced that one day Joe would don a Scotland jersey, proudly asked, "And how many teams do they have, son?"

"Just the one in my year," was Joe's triumphant reply.

The family were busily digesting that piece of news when in flounced twenty-year-old Elsie who now regarded herself, in the beauty stakes at least, as a stand-in for Audrey Hepburn – and to prove it she now had her sleek, dark hair cut short, *very* short. "Dad," she announced. "Now, I don't want you to be angry. And I don't want you to try and stop me, but I've decided that Leith and Nimmo's are just not big enough for me."

Tom was used to Elsie's flights of fancy, so he prepared to settle himself in his favourite armchair and hear her out.

Elsie had now taken up her preferred position centre-floor

(or centre-stage as she saw it) before she continued, "Russell and I have been talking and . . ."

"Who the devil is Russell?" enquired a bemused Crystal.

"He happens to be one of the youngest journeymen Nimmo's has ever produced and he and I are leaving that print workshop and heading for where our talents will be properly recognised." Flicking back her hair, she went on: "A place where we can expand and develop!"

"Oh my Gawd!" cried Patsy. "You're no going on that ten-pound passage thing to Australia, are ye?"

"Don't be ridiculous, Granny. Australia is a developing country. They just wouldn't be able to offer Russell and me the opportunity and the scope we need right now."

"So where *are* you going?" asked Joe, taking a full kick and flip-back at an imaginary ball.

"Bathgate!" To Elsie's dismay, this revelation dumbfounded everyone and she felt obliged to explain rapidly in clipped tones: "Bathgate is in West Lothian. And Russell assures me that it's earmarked to be *the* place of the future. Believe me, Bathgate will become the new industrial capital while dusty old Edinburgh will be left to wallow in its history. So what do you think, Dad?"

"We-ell," Tom began cautiously, "Myra telling me she was whisked out of bed last night by Peter Pan and then flown up to the moon to play with Snow White all sounds just so much more credible now!"

28

Patsy picked up the teapot and felt it before saying, "Still warm enough, Etta. Fancy a wee top-up?"

"I wouldn't mind," said Etta, before swinging round to look at the wall clock behind her. "Did you say Tom would be home by teatime?" Patsy nodded. "Well it's nearly cocoa time and where is he?" Patsy shrugged. "No word from him? Now that he's had a phone installed you'd think he could have rung you to say if they'd got away safely."

Getting to her feet stiffly, Patsy picked up her cup. "Yon thing did ring, but I've never used one of them before so I never answered it." Patsy sniffed disdainfully before going into the small scullery off the kitchen where she began to put water into the sink to wash the dishes. "Told our Myra when she came in," she hollered back, "to see who it was that it wanted to speak to. But you know how awkward she is. Never wants to do anything. Her excuse this time was that once it stops ringing it doesn't speak. Suppose it takes some kind of a huff."

Etta wondered whether she should try to show Patsy how the telephone worked. However, remembering when she'd tried to explain to her about the 'pill', she thought better of it.

Much to Patsy's chagrin, Etta was lighting up a cigarette when she came back into the room. Patsy tut-tutted, having agreed with Tom that after losing Dinah to 'the weed' – as he called tobacco – he didn't wish to see anybody smoking in his house.

"Must have been a hard day for Tom yesterday," remarked Etta, blowing her smoke upwards and hoping that would lessen its lethal effect. "Mind you, he's done real well by the bairns ever since . . ." She drew on her cigarette again, remembering that Patsy didn't mind speaking about what Dinah had done in her lifetime but not about the fact that she had died, so she quickly changed track by saying, "Aye, and it's thanks to Tom that Johnny and Frieda are now happily housed in their spanking-new home in Pirniefield."

Patsy chuckled, "And with not just one but *two* daughters. Thought it was real nice of Frieda to call the youngest Maria after Mary. Tom must have been pleased too that his mother was remembered again just as her funeral was over."

"Wonder what my Dinah would have thought of Elsie getting married to that printer guy, Russell?"

"Aye, but I think Tom was mightily relieved that they got hitched afore they left – even if he had to stump up for it."

"And d'you know, Etta, I don't think the poor soul got a penny change out of the hundred."

"Aye, but Patsy, why are they going to New Zealand?"

"You may well ask – and so did Tom. But Russell answered that Bathgate wasn't ready for him. Evidently they hadn't appreciated his genius. But he believes, and Elsie agrees, that a new country like New Zealand must be crying out for folk like him."

Etta laughed. "You know, Patsy, when Tess, your dear gullible Tess, got in tow with that stuffed shirt, Rupert, I thought she'd be the only one of your granddaughters to blindly worship her man. But here we are again. Mind you, Tess hasn't been so short-sighted that she'd get on a boat for New Zealand."

"No. And she's coped well with her two daughters."

"Aye, and now that Rupert has somehow worked it out that not only has the rhythm to be right – but that Tess's temperature also has to be spot-on – she hasn't got into his bad books by getting herself pregnant again."

Both women were beginning to laugh now. Each of them pictured poor, romantic Tess getting herself all dolled up in a black silk negligée and Rupert advancing towards her with a thermometer in his hand. They were wiping the tears from their eyes and were startled when Tom suddenly asked, "What's so funny?"

Patsy and Etta looked at each other before Patsy blurted out, "Oh, just that you won't be surprised, Tom, but . . ." She was now trying desperately to think of something seemly to tell him and then she remembered. "Oh, Tom, you know our Myra, who's now eleven but going on thirty?"

Tom nodded, "Aye, and her head's forever in the clouds."

"Well, now she believes she's clairvoyant and that the spirit of your Mammy came through to tell her that one day she would be a famous cook."

Etta, who had now diplomatically stubbed out her cigarette, remarked, "Aye, but wasn't it only last week that she managed to burn a hole in a pot – and she was only boiling water!"

Patsy was now through in the scullery making some tea for Tom. "How did you get on, son?"

It was quite a while before Tom gave an answer. "Fine. She just looked so young and vulnerable to be going to the other side of the world with a man . . ." He halted, trying to find words that wouldn't alarm Patsy, "who claims to have an amazing talent that has yet to be recognised." He paused again as he pondered. Then he amazed himself by saying, "And you know, I think they really *will* make it, not because of *his* shining light but because Elsie, like her mother, will dazzle."

Tom now looked about the room. "This place has been neglected these last few years."

"Aye, but Tom, you worked so hard getting Johnny's place looking like a palace that you haven't had . . ."

"I know, Patsy. But starting tomorrow I'm going to re-decorate this room."

Patsy laughed. "Don't think so."

"Oh but I will. This time, I don't care what one of my bairns needs, but this place is getting a face-lift."

"That right? But what if I told you that an English football scout's coming to talk to you about Joe tomorrow night?"

"Ah, then the decorating will have to begin after tomorrow."

Tom started the meal Patsy had set down in front of him but his thoughts were now all on Joe. Quick-witted, articulate Joe, with his easy charm and good looks, was so special. Tom pictured his ready smile and dark brown eyes. He excelled at school because he was perceptive and ever-alert. A born athlete, he'd been the youngest captain that the school football team had ever had. Tom now deliberated on his son's bloodline. Joe was the biological son of a black man. But what kind of man had engendered this smart, born leader? He wondered if the father would ever come looking for his son – or if Joe would leave them all behind and go off on his own seeking the answer to this enigma. Tom knew Joe would meet a lot of colour prejudice in his life but he also knew the lad would be perfectly able to deal with it.

Tom pushed his seat back and stood up. Joe, he knew, was at present playing for the junior team of Edina Hearts and now an English scout was coming to speak to him about his future. "Wonder which English team is interested in Joe. Please God," he prayed, "let them be from the north."

The sound of the door opening interrupted his thoughts. Turning towards the visitor, he was pleased to see it was his brother Archie. Tom had promised his mother that he would always look after him if anything happened to her and he'd been pleased to have Archie live with them. For his part, Archie was delighted to be included in Tom's family because there was always something going on and he was never made to feel unwanted.

It was obvious to them all that Archie's favourite among Tom's children was Crystal. Crystal would always have time to listen to what Archie had to say and she appeared genuinely interested in what he had to tell her about his work down at the British Ropes Despatch Depot, doing tasks most would find deadly boring. Everyone, however, could see how animated Archie could become when explaining to Crystal how he'd dispatched ropes to the Leith Whaling Station in South Georgia. "That's in the Antarctic," he would confide to her.

"Oor Crystal coming the day?" Archie asked, taking his seat on the couch.

Tom nodded. Like Archie, he thought there was something so very special about Crystal. Of all his children, it was Crystal who'd had the most eventful life over the past three years. He recalled her ever-increasing desire to have a baby. The more time passed without her falling pregnant, the greater her longing became. It wasn't until Tess went into hospital to have her second daughter and Crystal had been left to look after Davina for a fortnight that she seemed to relax. That seemed to have done the trick. Soon she was delighted to be having morning sickness. And from the day the doctor had confirmed the pregnancy, she'd worn a smock to let everybody know that she was expecting. Eventually, she gave birth to Tom's first grandson, David. Tom would never forget the sheer joy on her face when she showed him the baby – her own son, David. Her life then grew quite intense as she not only nursed her baby but also Granny Mary Glass, Tom's mother, when she was suddenly taken ill with pneumonia. Mary's death had left Crystal feeling so guilty, being unable to accept that the old lady was weary and had actually welcomed death as a friend. Then there had been the weekly trip to Bangour Psychiatric Hospital to visit Bing's mum. David was only five months old when Crystal realised she was three months pregnant again, and six months later Tom's second grandson, Alan, arrived.

When the football talent scout, Jack Brown, arrived and announced that he was the representative for First Division Fulham, despondency overtook Tom, who now had to accept it was just a matter of time until Joe left home. To add to Tom's disquiet, Jack Brown added that the Fulham manager was willing to give Joe a trial, with all expenses paid! On the other hand, Joe himself couldn't believe it. The offer was so much more than he had ever dared dream.

Before the scout left it was agreed that Joe, accompanied by Tom, would go to London for the trial.

On their arrival at Kings Cross, Tom and Joe were suitably impressed by being met at the station and being driven in style to the Fulham ground before being put up in a very comfortable hotel nearby.

The trial took place the following morning. Tom had mixed feelings – Joe seemed so very nervous and probably wouldn't play at his best. Yet his father, who was dreading the possibility that Joe might be leaving home, somehow wanted him to play well and see his dream come true.

Joe played marvellously and Tom couldn't hide his pride. But as the management wanted Joe to sign up there and then and begin his training down in London, Tom felt obliged, as Joe's guardian, to withhold his permission.

Taking Joe to one side Tom spoke solemnly to him, saying, "Son, Fulham is a great opportunity for you. But football is a short career and as you're bright I feel you should stay on at school in Edinburgh and get a Higher Leaving Certificate under your belt. That will carry you on to another career once you've finished chasing a ball around a field."

Joe shook his head. "But football is all I want to do – all I've ever wanted to do."

"I know. But you're a minor and I have the right to advise you to think again. Have I ever given you bad advice? Haven't I always acted in your best interests?" Joe nodded but said nothing. Tom went over and placed his hand on Joe's shoulder, "Look, son, in spite of what I've said, if you still persist – I'll sign." Joe shook his head and Tom smiled as he said, "Good. Now, son, believe me, three years will soon pass and I'm sure Fulham's offer will still be on the table when it has."

29

Tom was staring out of the window into his back garden, thinking that now he'd spruced up the whole of the house over the last three years it was high time to do some work on his garden. Some landscaping, he felt, would be best. And maybe he could get a bench and bird bath. When all that had been achieved, it would make such a nice place to relax and reminisce. After all, he was now getting on a bit. Before he could scold himself for thinking about taking time to sit in the garden when old age overtook him, he realised that Joe was standing beside him. "Didn't hear you come in, son," he said, putting his hand round Joe's shoulder. Joe smiled. In the past three years he'd sprouted to six-foot-two and now quite dwarfed Tom's five-foot-ten.

"How do you think it'll go today, Dad?"

Tom realised Joe was feeling nervous. Well into the wee small hours, they'd discussed what would be best for the lad. At eighteen, he now had his Higher Leaving Certificate and Tom would cheerfully have financed him through university or college. He even suggested that Joe might try for a trade. But Joe's heart was still set on playing football and Jack Brown, the Fulham scout, was coming back today. In Tom's eyes the only drawback for Joe (if he did go to Fulham) was that it was away in London! It would mean Joe leaving the family behind – the family where he'd always been accepted. He'd been treated no better and no worse than any of his siblings. How would he cope without their support?

For Joe's part, he'd grown to love Tom deeply during the past year. He was now sufficiently worldly wise and mature to appreciate how difficult it must have been for Tom to come back from the war and find that his wife, Joe's mother, had had an affair. And to add to that humiliation the evidence, for the whole world to see, lay in the mixed-race child sitting on the carpet.

Joe remained wholly unaware of the blazing row and physical attack on Dinah that took place when Tom arrived home from the POW camp. He'd been too young to have any clear memory of sitting in the gang-hut with Crystal, who'd vowed she'd never let anyone "kill" him – as if Tom had it in him to kill anyone! He didn't even know that Sam Campbell, when only a child – but a wily one – had negotiated with Tom the terms Crystal demanded before she would return home with Joe.

There might well have been a smaller crowd to see off the Queen when she departed from Edinburgh, thought Tom, as he and the family assembled on the platform to wave Joe goodbye.

It had been such a quick four weeks since Joe signed his contract with Fulham. Tom had thought, when he waved Elsie off to New Zealand, that she would be the only one of the brood to fly the nest completely. Now here they were seeing Joe off to London. Tom couldn't explain why he felt even more bereft about Joe's departure. Could it be (as he suspected) that they wouldn't see much of him when he became a star? Or was it that when Joe found his feet in London he would feel happier down there and forget all

MILLIE GRAY

about Restalrig? Or was it that he might some day feel confident enough in the big world to go and seek out his natural father?

The guard had his whistle in his mouth and his flag held aloft. Joe grabbed Patsy first and cuddled her, saying, "Bye, Granny. I'll see you soon – honest."

As he let her go, Patsy thought that one of the best things she'd ever done in her life was to stop Dinah, her darling daughter, from having aborted Joe. She brushed a tear from her eye, knowing that this was a secret she'd take to her grave.

Now Joe was saying goodbye to Crystal and her two sons, David and Alan. Holding them close, he realised there were no adequate words he could say to Crystal, who'd played such a crucial role in his upbringing – even financing him in whatever way he required – and not seeing her regularly was going to be so hard to bear.

The whistle was now blowing and Joe turned to Tom who'd opened the door of the carriage and was urging him to get on board. "Quick, son. Jump in."

"But Dad, I have . . ."

"No, you don't! Just do well, son. That's all I ask. But please . . ." The train was now leaving the station and as it gained momentum Tom ran along the platform shouting to Joe, who was leaning out of the window. "Please, son. Don't forget me." But Joe never heard a word that Tom said. All he could do was to return Tom's frantic waves of goodbye.

30

The flat in Jameson Place was in turmoil. Crystal had been trying on several cocktail-length dresses that she'd borrowed from her sister Tess and her pals Molly and Ena. "What do you think, Bing?" she asked, as she twirled in a frothy, shocking-pink tulle dress – a dress that, she knew, did nothing for her or her crooked leg.

Bing laid down the paper he was reading. He wished now that when he'd been told he'd been selected as Employee of the Year he'd asked them simply to forward his certificate by post rather than have it presented to him at the black-tie ball in the prestigious Assembly Rooms of Edinburgh's George Street.

The problem was: what should they each wear? For Bing there was only the expense of hiring a dinner suit. But Crystal should really attend in an evening dress. Such a thing she simply didn't possess and they certainly couldn't afford to splash out on one. Right now, every penny was a prisoner since they were saving to buy a better house – a home that would have a front and back door as well as a garden. "Well," her husband eventually responded, "other peoples' frocks are just not right for you. A long dress would be better."

Crystal knew he was thinking that a full-length evening gown would hide her legs. Not that he personally would feel embarrassed but he knew just how much it would affect her.

Aware of her despondency, Bing went over and put his

arms around her. "Look, to hang with saving all our spare dosh for the house. You go over to the Leith Provi tomorrow and get yourself the dress you need."

She supposed that must be the right thing to do. It was important to her that Bing's diligence and hard work had been recognised and that she should be kitted out properly. And what was even more important to her was that the certificate should be handed over to him at a posh affair and not posted to him second class.

As soon as she arrived at the Ladies' Section of the Great Junction Street store with Tess in tow, she felt elated. She'd never seen such beautiful dresses – and in all sizes and colours.

Tess, being Tess, explained in her most elegant manner to the shop assistant what was required.

Four dresses duly arrived but it was the lilac one that Crystal instantly fell in love with. She didn't even bother to try on any of the others. "Oh," she gasped, proudly parading around the room. "Will we just take it, Tess?"

"Hmmm," said Tess, glancing at the assistant. "Perhaps we could try some others."

The young girl had just left when Crystal twirled around in the lilac dress again. "Look, Tess, this is exactly the dress I want."

"I know that," Tess replied. "But look at the price of it."

"So?"

Tess now ushered Crystal to one side and began to whisper in her ear, "Look, when I have to go to a dinner or dance, Rupert insists that I get a dress from here out on *appro*. You know, on approval. I wear it to the do – taking care not to get it stained or torn. The next day I air it and then I take it back, saying it wasn't quite to my husband's liking."

Crystal gasped as the notion fully dawned on her. She could really and truly go to the ball dressed like Cinderella without spending some of their precious savings. Yes, she could. Beyond taking the dress out on appro, all she'd have to do was buy lace mittens. And Tess would lend her silver shoes and a matching handbag!

Granny Patsy, who would be caring for the boys, arrived an hour early. She was so excited about Crystal getting all dolled up and going to a ball. Her very first ball!

And when Crystal, resplendent in the lilac gown, eventually came out of the bedroom, Granny Patsy gasped and her eyes filled with tears. "Oh, hen," she said, "you look just like Princess Margaret. Now, don't fine feathers make fine birds?"

Bing – who'd said he felt like a penguin in a straitjacket in his evening suit – was at first quite tongue-tied. When finally he did manage to speak, he stammered, "Oh, d-darling, I've never ever seen you looking lovelier."

He went over to embrace her but she put up her hand saying, "No. Now, don't crush me. Like Cinderella, the dress goes back tomorrow."

Granny and Bing both started to laugh as the doorbell sounded and Crystal said, "Hope that's not a horse-drawn carriage."

"No. It'll just be your Dad. He drove me down here. That's why I was so early. He said he'd some papers to deliver to the school first. But he'd come on here later. Said he couldn't let you go to your first ball without having a good look-see."

When the taxi drew up at the floodlit entrance to the

Assembly Rooms, Bing alighted first and was careful to assist Crystal out. Entering the front entrance hall, Crystal was completely spellbound. Never had she seen such splendour as those magnificent sparkling chandeliers. Immediately they were directed by the liveried ushers towards the cloakrooms. There they'd leave their coats and Crystal would have an opportunity to freshen her make-up.

Dinner was the first item on the programme but once they realised they were to sit at the top of Table Two, so that Bing could readily approach the top table to receive his prize, Crystal began to panic. There were just so many glasses and the cutlery went in all directions, up the way and sideways on the table in front of her. How could she possibly know which fork, knife or spoon she should be using? As her panic gave way to terror, a large jovial woman sat down beside her. "Hello there," she said chirpily. "I'm Evelyn Lamb and I'm just here for the beer, you know. It's my husband who's getting presented."

"Same here," Crystal replied, gradually feeling more relaxed.

"Mind you," continued Evelyn, "it's nice to get invited to a free dinner." Evelyn leant forward, grabbed a bottle of red wine and proceeded to fill one of the glasses in front of her, "And the booze is on the house too. Shall I fill up your glass?"

Crystal shook her head but Bing now bent forward with a glass in his hand and replied, "I don't mind if I do."

After Crystal declined the offer of wine, Evelyn had replaced the bottle, but when Bing said he'd like to indulge, she seized the bottle again and, leaning over Crystal, began to pour some red wine into Bing's glass. Unfortunately, her husband arrived at that moment and, giving her ample bottom a sound slap, announced, "Silly cookie, you are. You're . . ."

Crystal screamed as Evelyn dropped the wine bottle and half its contents into her lap. Immediately a waiter rushed over with a napkin and tried to sponge up the liquid that by now was trickling down into Crystal's shoes. "Blast!" he said "Red wine's notorious. You just can't get the stain out. Hope your dress is insured."

A tearful Crystal blurted out in reply, "It's on appro!"

The waiter – who hadn't a clue as to what appro meant – thought it was probably the name of her insurance company and commented, "Now, aren't you the lucky one!"

The remainder of the evening could well have been a disaster had everyone not been so very sympathetic to Crystal. And when Bing was called forward to be presented, not only with his certificate but also with a Jenner's gift voucher for twenty pounds, Crystal felt so proud she didn't care that the dress was ruined.

When eventually they were leaving, the doorman asked if he'd call them a taxi as the rain was now pouring down. Crystal looked at Bing before declining the offer. A walk in the rain they were used to, and as for the ball gown . . . well, a little bit of water might even help.

Unfortunately, cemetery staff were required to work to a duty rota. Accordingly, they had alternate weekends off. Bing, who happened to be weekend-on, had tried hard to get someone to swap shifts with him but none of the others had obliged. They were all quite miffed that he'd been selected Employee of the Year.

It was three o'clock in the morning when Crystal and Bing finally fell asleep. The story of what had happened to the dress and all the excitement of the dinner and ball had to be related to Granny Patsy before she herself could go to sleep on her makeshift bed on the settee. So when the alarm went off at seven-thirty, Bing felt like chucking the clock out of the window; but after some consideration, which included realising how it might look if the Employee of the Year hadn't gone to work because of a hangover, he decided to get up.

As soon as he stepped out of the stair and into the street, he was surprised to find the pavements covered in thick white frost. "Brrr," he shivered, pulling up his coat collar. Then, despite the hoar frost, he spied a bus coming and immediately decided that, rather than walk to work as he usually did, he would catch the bus.

Bing had just left when both Crystal and Granny Patsy sat down to their breakfast. "Granny, are you in a hurry to get home?" asked Crystal, through a mouthful of toast and marmalade. Patsy shook her head. "Good! Now do you think you could watch the boys while I run along to the store with the dress?"

"But I thought you said you were going to pay for it. Come on, Crystal, you don't really expect them to take it back in the state it's in?"

Crystal smiled. "Of course not. But I thought they might know where I could get it cleaned."

"Have you gone mad, Crystal? You don't clean things you're going to bucket."

"I know that, but I thought that if it would clean I might be able to sell it. Okay, it's a long shot but I just might recoup something."

* * *

As luck would have it, when Crystal arrived at the Co-op on the dot of nine, it was the buyer who was on the floor. Taking the dress out of the bag, Crystal took a deep breath before saying, "I got this dress out on appro . . ."

The woman seized the dress and her face grew red with rage. "This happens every week. But we've now got a scheme that'll put an end to it," she screamed, flinging the dress across the room. "From now on, evening dresses will only be allowed out on appro on a Monday and returned by Wednesday." She snorted into Crystal's face before adding, "And if they are not returned by six o'clock on Wednesday, then they'll be deemed to have been sold. Is that quite clear?"

Crystal, who had tried to interrupt several times, now quietly said, "If you will just let me explain."

"Explain!" bellowed the woman, who skipped over the floor to kick the dress. "What's there to explain?"

"You're quite right. I did take out the dress in the hope of wearing it to a ball last night. And it was my intention to return it to you on Monday saying it was not suitable." Though the woman tried to interrupt again, Crystal silenced her with a dismissive wave of her hand. "But when the dress got saturated with wine, I decided to come in and pay for it. Here!" Crystal took out a five pound note and placed it on the counter. "What I really wanted to ask you was this: is there some way the dress might be cleaned?"

The woman sniffed contemptuously. "Our drycleaners can work miracles," she went over and picked up the dress to inspect it again, "but they are quite unable to cope with the impossible."

Crystal nodded. "Thank you so much for trying to help," she said sweetly, hoping that the woman realised how negative she'd been. "And now," she stated firmly, "if you'd give me my five bob change I'll be on my way."

She was about to leave the store when the woman came rushing after her with the dress. "You forgot your ball gown, madam."

Crystal stared at the officious shop assistant before responding, "No. You please have it. I think with the mess it's in it would suit you better!"

She'd just left the store and had begun to walk along Great Junction Street to do some shopping when she noticed a police van next to the store and two constables running into the shop. "Surely," she thought, "she hasn't sent the police after me!" Not being certain, Crystal broke into a run until she reached the top of the Kirkgate, where she went on to Bowman's the pork butcher to buy some sausages.

Half an hour had passed before she finally turned into Jameson Place. Then her heart sank. That blooming police van was parked at the bottom of her stair. Her first instinct was to run away, but then she accepted that what she'd done might have been dishonest but, after all, she *had* paid for the dress.

She wasn't at all surprised to find that the front door of her home was open. What did surprise her was that one of the constables was comforting her Granny who was weeping uncontrollably.

Immediately Crystal went over and pulled the policeman's arms away from her grandmother. "Why are you upsetting an old woman about a bloody frock?"

"Oh, Crystal," her Granny sobbed as she rose from the chair and made Crystal sit down. "They're here to tell us that your Bing fell getting off the bus. He slipped on the icy pavement, and banged his head. He's in Leith hospital. Fatal, they say it is. But he's no deid yet. On a life-support thing!"

As Crystal sat by Bing's hospital bed, she was aware that the distant voice speaking to her was that of her father. But what he was saying she didn't hear and it wasn't until he tapped her firmly on the shoulder that his voice became clear. "Crystal," he urged, "the doctor is speaking to you."

Crystal looked from her father towards the young registrar. "Why," she wondered, "is he wringing his hands? And why does he look so concerned?"

"Mrs – er – Mrs Crosby," he stammered, "your husband is now what we term . . . brain-dead." Crystal looked at Bing who was still warm and obviously still alive. She turned her gaze back to the doctor who explained, "It's only the machine that's keeping him alive and it might be best to turn it off. Do we have your permission? Perhaps you'd like it left on until, let's say – his family have come?"

She shook her head. "There's only his mother but she'd be unable to cope here. I'll break it to her next week."

"In that case, Mrs Crosby . . ."

Crystal put up her hand. "Please leave us, Doctor. Just for a few minutes. That's all I ask."

After the doctor had left, Tom asked, "D'you want the boys to come and say goodbye to Bing?"

"No!" she cried out. "I think it's best they remember him as he was last night," she sobbed, laying her head on Bing's chest and looking directly into his face, "Darling, you said you never wanted to be kept alive unnaturally. So will I say they can switch their machine off?" She closed her eyes and then sought her father's hand. "Tell them to do it now."

She waited with Tom until Bing was no longer with them and then they left the hospital together. "How do you tell kids of six and seven that their wonderful father has . . .?" She couldn't continue and all Tom could do was to squeeze her hand.

The following Monday was even more difficult than the Saturday had been. By Monday, nature's anaesthetics had begun to wear off. And now Crystal and Tom were up at the mortuary in the Cowgate. The attendant politely explained that it was necessary for formal identification to be carried out where a post-mortem was required.

Crystal and Tom had just completed the upsetting formalities and were out of the building when two police officers came bounding up the steps.

They were about to pass Crystal and Tom when one stopped and held out his hand to Tom. "Mr Glass," Sam Campbell said, shaking Tom's hand warmly. "What on earth brings you here, of all places?"

Crystal was so upset that at first she wasn't even aware of Sam's presence and all Tom could say was, "Crystal's husband had a fatal accident on Saturday. We were just identifying him."

Sam stepped back. "I'm so sorry, Crystal." But as she was quite unheeding he turned instead to Tom. "You know, it's said that this job hardens you," and Sam's open hand gestured towards Crystal, "but when you see someone you grew up with so shattered . . ."

Tom nodded and steered Crystal into the street and over to his parked car.

At first, Crystal was so completely dazed that she acceded to anything her father suggested. He immediately moved both her and the boys to Restalrig. Then he arranged Bing's funeral for Friday, instead of the following Monday, believing it better to get such things over as quickly as possible for Crystal's sake. He was aware that Friday would cause a problem for Joe, who had to be available for Fulham's Saturday match. And even if Joe had sought permission to attend his brother-in-law's funeral, it would have been denied. The only funeral he could attend, with or without Fulham's permission, was his own!

Nonetheless, Joe turned up at the crematorium with just thirty minutes to spare. The family eagerly crowded round him, wanting to hear how he was faring and they showed their obvious disappointment when he said he'd have to rush off to catch the four o'clock London train.

Downhearted they may have been but they all trooped down to Waverley to wave him off before congregating at Tom's for the customary boiled ham tea.

When only the family were left, Tess asked, "You meaning to put Crystal and the boys up here, Dad?"

Tom nodded.

"I'm quite happy to have the boys with me in my room," said Archie, looking about him for signs of approval to this suggestion.

Crystal stood up and gestured to David and Alan that they should collect their things. "Thank you, Archie. That's very kind of you. But I'm going home."

"No. No," Tom countermanded. "For you and the boys, home is with me now."

Shaking her head, Crystal walked over and lifted her coat from the coat-stand. "Thank you, Dad. But no thanks. They're my children and I'll bring them up in our wee flat, pokey as you all think it is, and that's an end to it."

"But Crystal, are you forgetting that Bing wasn't superannuated?" Rupert reminded her, "You'll only have a widow's pension. No private one. Life will be a struggle."

"Rupert, my life has never been anything else but a bloody struggle. I have all the experience needed for this struggle – so the bairns and I are going home to our cosy wee flat in Jameson Place."

Granny Patsy knew how determined Crystal could be but she thought she might change things by saying, "You'll have to go out and work, hen."

"I *do* work. I have my wee job as a dinner lady at Leith Academy Primary and on that – along with whatever else I may get – we'll get by."

Tom knew they were beaten but he went on regardless, while Crystal rolled her eyes up to look at the ceiling. "Andy and I were thinking," he said, "you're bright, Crystal. But you need educating. Night school is where you should start. Get a couple of O-grades."

"Dad! Can we think about all that tomorrow – or next year – or preferably never," Crystal snorted, unable to conceal her impatience. "Right now, I'm tired. My boys are tired. We want to go home. Are you going to drive us?"

Tom lifted his car keys from the sideboard.

The three mature students exited from Telford College at Crewe Road in the north of Edinburgh. Once outwith the college grounds, Sylvia asked, "Well, Crystal, how did you rate tonight's taster class?"

"I like Modern Studies and I think Mr Durkin should manage to make the subject really interesting when we start in September."

"So do I," agreed Hilda. "And I particularly liked it when he told us to watch *Panorama* and *World In Action* because all we'd then need to do to pass our Highers was to buy *The Observer* on a Sunday."

"Thank goodness for that," remarked Sylvia, "because I checked it out, ladies, and all we need is two Highers, one preferably in English, and an O-grade in Maths. Then Moray House will accept us as trainee primary school teachers."

"So next year at this time we could all be signing up for Moray House," Hilda said gloatingly.

They'd now walked down to Ferry Road to catch a No.1 bus back to Leith when Crystal suddenly announced, "I don't think I want to go in for this teaching lark. My Dad's a teacher and he's pushing me too hard to be one too. 'You'll need a career with a pension at the end of it,' he keeps saying. What he really means is I was lucky to get one man so there's no chance of me getting another, especially as I come with baggage – you know, my two sons – so I guess I'll be working for the rest of my life!"

"Here's you, Crystal, talking about getting another man," quipped Hilda.

"I'm not looking. Honestly I'm not," protested Crystal.

"Look! Just listen for a second. There's a dance this weekend in aid of Salvesen's Boys' Club football team. So how about . . . ?"

"Hilda! How about you stop trying to pair me off? That last dance you got me to go to was enough to put me off for life. I still get nightmares about it!"

"What happened?" asked Sylvia, indicating that their bus was approaching the roundabout and that they'd better make a run for it.

They were on the bus and trying to get their breath back when Crystal panted, "What happened? I'll tell you what happened. I went in there, a quiet wee soulless widow woman – the first time I'd really been out on my own since Bing – and suddenly every woman in the hall was hanging on to her man for fear I was about to devour him."

Sylvia started to laugh and two other women who were on the bus moved their seats so they could listen to the story.

"I've never been so embarrassed in all my life. Jacky Scott, who used to work with me in the Bond, came over and asked me to dance and we'd just taken our places on the floor when his wife tapped my shoulder and announced: 'Sorry, pal, but this is a wife's-touch dance and you can touch whoever you like as long as you get yer grubby hands aff my stupid man!' *Her* man? I wouldn't have had him in a lucky bag!" Now all the audience were laughing. "And," Crystal went on, "from then on it was all downhill. Especially when it was half-time and the bun fight was in progress. Would you believe it? Six women I knew, who were serving up the sausage rolls, sandwiches and buns, all pretended I was invisible. Deliberately wanted me to starve. Even when I stood right in front of one of them and said, 'I'd like a sandwich,' she snapped back at me, 'No if ye ken what side your bread's buttered on.'"

"Since your husband died, have you always found that women are nervous when you're around?"

"Aye. What an eye-opener it's been. And the men! They're even worse. They all think you're missing something and offer to see you all right."

"You're joking?" Hilda sneered.

"I'm not. Even the blooming church elder delivers my communion card at eleven o'clock at night. Had the cheek to ask me if I was lonely and going to bed soon!" Crystal started to laugh. "But see, the last time he came it was a night-school night and my Granny Patsy always watches the boys and stays all night as well."

One of the women who'd moved closer to listen said, "Could you hurry the story up please? I'm getting off when the bus turns into Great Junction Street."

Crystal nodded. "Well, didn't I send my eighty-two-year-old Granny Patsy to the door in her Dinky curlers and without her teeth. Talk about giving him a fright! Vaulted down the stairs he did, when Granny asked him in for a cup of cocoa."

Twenty minutes later, Crystal opened her front door and stole quietly into the living room. Granny Patsy was sitting in front of the television, fast asleep with a cup of half-drunk cocoa in her hand. Gently lifting the cup away and then bending over to switch off the television, Crystal wondered if she wasn't putting too much strain on Patsy. After all, she was eighty-two years of age and riddled with arthritis. But she never complained, no matter how often Crystal asked for help with minding the boys.

"Oh you're back, hen. How'd you get on?" Patsy asked quite suddenly.

"I really liked the Modern Studies better than Monday night's English class."

"Aye, but your Dad says you need the English if you're to get on." Crystal tutted. "You can tut, my lass, and I grant you you've done well since you lost Bing." Crystal smiled inwardly, thinking how her Granny always made it sound as if she had somehow been careless and mislaid Bing. "Done well by the boys too, so you have. Now, do you know? For the first six months, I thought you were never going to get on with your life. But you've surprised us all."

"Granny, ken how I was going to take the boys on a good holiday next year?" Patsy nodded. "Well, Dad says he'd go with us to Cornwall. Evidently you can put your car on the train at Waverley Station and drive it off at Exeter. The boys would love that. Going on a train and then being driven around in Dad's new car."

"So? What's the problem?"

"Well, it's so expensive. But . . . no, you've done enough looking after the boys without me asking you to do more."

"Look, are you saying I'm past it? That I'm decrepit? I love minding they lads and they love me. We get on real well thegither. Now, what were you going to say before you let your belly rumble?"

Crystal giggled. "Oh, Granny, it's just that I could get two nights of night-shift at the weekends as an auxiliary nurse in the City Hospital. Pays real well with double-time on Sunday – but that would mean . . ."

"I'll be fine. Just make sure you bring me a *Woman's*

Weekly and a *People's Friend*. Great stories in those magazines, so there is. And the recipes usually work out – though not always."

Crystal smiled, knowing it was Granny that didn't always follow the recipes quite correctly, like last week when she mistakenly substituted baking powder for cornflour, but all she said was, "Granny, how would you like a nice hot cup of cocoa?"

By the time June came to an end, Crystal had been working for five weeks in the City Hospital. She'd only been given two hours' training with the time being taken up on how to push a bed-pan under someone's bottom, to hand out sick bowls and do a bed-bath.

The ward she'd been assigned to was for those with lung diseases – half of whom were terminal. But Crystal liked the work, probably because the night staff nurse, Janet Green, was what the patients called a real gem. It wasn't just her patients' welfare she looked after but also that of her staff, right down to the lowly auxiliaries. As soon as she found out that Crystal was a widow with two children and had spent the last year getting her O-grades and would be tackling two or even three Highers starting in September, the staff nurse took her under her wing. Calling Crystal into the ward office one Sunday night when there was a little bit of spare time, she said, "Now, I've been thinking, and before you say anything I won't put you off doing your Highers, but you *do* have the potential to be a splendid nurse and you should think about doing your training."

Sighing inwardly because she felt it would be nice if people would only let her decide what she was going to do with her own life, Crystal replied, "I don't know. You see,

I'm not sure. And to be honest, I have to do what would best suit my boys."

Janet nodded her head, fully accepting that it would take time to get Crystal to see that nursing was right for her. And to help her along she said, "Oh, you know how short-staffed we'll be next week – so could you do some extra nights?" Crystal readily gave her agreement, knowing she could do with the money. "And that new patient that came in today . . ."

"I haven't been to his bed yet," said Crystal.

"Yes, I know. But, you see, he's terminal – yet very restless. I feel something's bothering him. If you have any spare time, like now, could you possibly look in on him and perhaps have a wee chat with him? John Campbell's his name."

On hearing the name John Campbell, a shiver ran down Crystal's spine. She couldn't explain why. John Campbell was such a common name – but still she felt uneasy.

Slipping quietly behind the screen surrounding the bed, Crystal looked down at the face of the dying man and knew she'd been right to feel uneasy. The man in the bed was Sam Campbell's father, Johnny Campbell, who had deserted his family away back in time.

Johnny seemed to sense that someone was looking down on him and he murmured, "Rachel?"

Before Crystal could speak, the screen moved and a priest crept in. "How is he tonight, nurse? Still as troubled?"

Crystal nodded silently. Now she was in a dilemma. Should she tell the priest that she knew what was troubling Johnny? She was sure that he wanted to see his family again before he died. Perhaps even to speak with them. Even try to explain why he'd left them. But was it her business to interfere? Deciding to leave well alone, she patted Johnny's hand and bade the priest goodnight.

The following Tuesday was one of the extra nights Crystal had agreed to work and when she went in to tend Johnny she was disturbed by his continuing agitation. She resolved then to tell his priest who the patient was and about the family matters of which nobody seemed to be aware.

The following night, when Crystal was making her way back from her break, she was delighted to see Carrie Campbell about to leave the hospital. "Hello, Carrie," she called out.

However, it was twenty-four hours later, when Crystal again went in to tend Johnny, that she was surprised to see Sam sitting by his father's bed. From time to time, Johnny removed the oxygen mask so that he could gasp out some words that were only audible to Sam.

It was just before Crystal was going off duty that Johnny Campbell died. Sam, the son whom he'd deserted, had stayed with him to the very end. Some time later, he silently rose to his feet, preparing to leave the hospital, but was approached by Janet, the staff nurse, who had astutely worked out that Crystal and Sam had known one another at some time in the past. Quickly she suggested, as it was nearly the end of their shift, that Crystal should accompany him home.

Once outside, Sam asked, "Where to?"

"At school times, my Granny looks after the children. But right now they're with my father, since he's on holiday. And that lets me get a sleep. Look, Sam, I could easily stay with you until . . ."

"Don't feel like going to my own place."

"Then why not come home with me? I'll make you some breakfast."

In the four weeks since Sam Campbell had come back into her life, Crystal felt she'd been truly reborn. Every second night was spent at Jameson Place. Sam had been very keen for her and the boys to visit his bungalow in Craigentinny Avenue North but Crystal declined, not yet having plucked up the courage to tell her father and granny about Sam and herself. "The boys," she explained to Sam, "might just spill the beans before I'm ready for the consequences."

By now school had taken up again, with Granny Patsy resuming her nightly duties of looking after the boys since Tom was back at his teaching.

After bedding the boys and before sitting down to have a cup of tea, Patsy decided one evening to do a spot of tidying up. The bathroom was always where the worst muddle was and Granny was busily picking up tooth brushes or face cloths and putting them where they should be when she was more than a little surprised to find a recently used Gillette razor. All night long Patsy lay, tossing and turning on Crystal's bed, trying to figure out whose it was and why it was there.

Eventually morning arrived – with the unwanted answer when Crystal arrived home with Sam Campbell who'd also been on night shift.

Diplomatically, Patsy ignored the shocking revelation (as she saw it) and was grateful to leave for her own home.

Crystal was well aware that, before going home, Patsy would visit her father and tell him what was going on. She also deduced that Tom would be visiting her just as soon as he finished his classes.

Thankfully neither David nor Alan had yet come home from school when Tom appeared.

"What in the name of heaven is going on?" was his opening gambit. "Are you mad or something? Your Granny belongs to the old school. She's shocked that you of all people should go crazy."

"Never been saner," was Crystal's retort.

"Crystal," shouted Tom, losing his self-control and grabbing her by the arm. "Why are you behaving like a Leith Street tart? Have you no shame? No sense of propriety?"

"Shame? What have I done that's so awful? So wrong?"

"Having Sam Campbell stay here is no less than fornication!"

"Oh, Dad, I do like that old-fashioned word, *fornication*. But might I ask you this? As Sam isn't married and as I am a widow – who are we hurting, other than yourself and your Victorian moral code?"

Tom sank down on the chair where Granny Patsy always sat. "Crystal, I know you're lonely," he began. "I've been so lonely too, ever since your Mum died, but you have to put your own personal desires aside for the sake of those you're responsible for – in short you must lead an exemplary life."

"And do you honestly believe that Sam Campbell, whom you know, would in any way harm my boys?" Crystal's voice now cracked with quiet anger. "And, what's even more hurtful is you thinking I would allow anyone to abuse them?"

Tom got up and walked over to Crystal. Then, lifting her chin up so that he could look her straight in the eyes, he pleaded: "Crystal, all your life you've chased this man. He never gave you a second look in the past. Bing knew how you hankered after Sam but he married you and you made a go of it." Crystal gave a dismissive shrug that infuriated Tom, but he controlled his anger as best he could. "And tell me this. What's so special about Sam Campbell? And why are you, a daughter of mine, lowering yourself by allowing him to share your bed?"

Realising that there was a distinct possibility that the argument could end in words being said that might cause a rift between her father and herself, Crystal moderated her tone. "Dad, please don't worry," she urged, gently patting his shoulder. "Sam and I are older now and I'm sure it will all work out for us."

Rocking her gently back and forward, Tom quietly pleaded, "Och, darling, just tell me what it is that's so special about him? What does he do for you that no other man can offer you?"

Taking a very deep breath before releasing herself from her father's arms, Crystal calmly explained, "It's really quite simple, Daddy. He makes me sing in the morning!"